Gather your family together,
whether around the tree on Christmas Eve
or during the drive to visit relatives for the holidays.

The Magic Sleigh Bell *can be enjoyed in*
a single reading or a few pages each evening
at bedtime in the days leading up to Christmas.

However you choose to experience
the enchanting story told in
The Magic Sleigh Bell,
it is sure to become a Yuletide tradition
in your home.

The Magic Sleigh Bell

by

W. PETER ELLIOTT

ELFUNBEL INC.

Published by
Elfunbel Inc.
P.O. Box 281
Kingston, Ontario
Canada, K7L 4V8

Printed in Canada, 1997

Canadian Cataloguing in Publication Data

Elliott, W. Peter, 1954-
    The magic sleigh bell

ISBN 0-9680959-0-9

    1. Christmas--Juvenile fiction. I. Title.

PS8559.L549M34 1996   jC813'.54   C96-900515-6
PZ7.E466Ma 1996

To my wife for your love and assistance. To my sons for your inspiration. To my mother and late father for a lifetime of encouragement.

TABLE OF CONTENTS

CHAPTER ONE

The Discovery

here was definitely something out of place in the string of lights above the garage.

"A red one, a clear one. A red one, a clear one. A red one, a red one! Ah-hah!" exclaimed Natalie to no one in particular. "Two red ones in a row." She would have to point this out to Mr. and Mrs. Tremblay the next time she saw them.

All the neighbourhood homes were adorned with decorative lighting.

Except hers.

Even though it was now well into December, the autumn clean-up chores of her family's home were only being finished today.

She was supposed to be helping her brother and father rake up the leaves, but it was more fun to admire everyone else's holiday decorations. Christmas and all its festivities had been first and foremost in her mind for the past couple of weeks.

"Hey, Dad! Are we finished or what?" cried out her 10-year-old brother, Travis, his cheeks rosy with youthful enthusiasm.

"Not yet," their father replied. "There are more leaves right to the corner."

The cold winds penetrated Jim Kirkland's sweater and numbed his fingertips. He was at the top of the extension ladder, necessary for reaching the eavestroughs which overflowed with fallen autumn leaves.

Still retaining some of the beautiful colours they had turned to before falling off the towering maple trees, the leaves achieved flight one final time as Jim scooped them out and onto the lawn.

"Look out, Nat, or you'll get clobbered!" instructed Travis, brandishing the rake with the confidence of someone who had finally conquered yard equipment still taller than he was.

"It's Natalie, N-A-T-A-L-I-E, not Nat. I don't re-spond to nicknames!" an indignant Natalie countered. She was a bubbly, optimistic 7-year-old, who had a growing confidence in herself and her place in the world.

"Yeah, yeah, right...just bag the leaves before it starts snowing." He liked to tease his sister, but it was in good fun, as he really did like her.

She was admiring all the colours of the leaves as she stuffed them into the plastic bag, when the momentary glint of something shiny caught Travis' eye.

"Hey, hold on. What was that?" he asked, as he came over and started searching through the leaves.

"What's what?" said Natalie, her eyes growing with wonderment as her brother pulled out a short piece of leather strap with a small, single enclosed bell attached to it. He shook it, but it made no sound because the inside was packed with dirt and dried leaves.

"I wonder where this came from?" queried Travis, as he wiped away some of the caked-on mud, revealing a shiny chrome-like surface.

"I know...it's probably off Santa's sleigh!" proclaimed Natalie. She was quick to relate everything to the holiday season. "It must have fallen off last year when he landed on the roof to deliver the presents. It's been lying in the *eavesdrops* ever since, and now we've found it!"

"They're called eavestroughs, Miss Know-It-All, and I hardly think that this old piece of junk is from a flying sleigh, because as everyone knows..."

"Okay, that's all of it," interrupted their father, as he descended the ladder. "You kids finish bagging the last pile, and I'll put the ladder back in the garage."

"Oh, Daddy, guess what Travis found...one of Santa's sleigh bells!" exclaimed Natalie, as her father lifted the ladder onto his shoulder and headed off for the garage.

He made no reply, as he didn't want to think about anything to do with Christmas. Out of work for nearly a year, he was beginning to doubt his decision to give priority to his family over his job. The more worried he became, the less patience he had with the kids, and it took an extra effort to not speak harshly to them sometimes. It was better not to say anything.

Travis and Natalie, each wondering about the origins of their unusual find, watched silently as their father disappeared around the side of the house. Lost in thought, they dutifully raked and bagged the leaves for the trip to the composting depot.

Travis had stuffed the bell into his back pocket and forgotten about it by the time they had put away the rake and dashed out of the cold, into the house.

Their father had surprised them with a cup of hot chocolate to warm them up, though he did not stay around to share it with them. Instead, he had gone to the makeshift desk in the basement to review his job application file and the "CAREERS" section of the weekend newspaper.

Natalie was busy with her colouring book, and Travis was thinking of his next hockey game when he shifted in his chair and felt the bell in his pocket. He pulled it out and studied it for a while. He was about to make a sarcastic remark to his sister, when he suddenly had second thoughts and decided not to. It wasn't like him to pass up an opportunity to tease her, but when he thought about this little bell and whether it had been in the eavestrough...well then, if so, how did it get there?

It was rather small, and as he looked closer he noticed the delicate etching of a snowflake pattern on the bell's surface. Trying again to ring it, he inspected the caked-on mud as he got up from the table and went to the sink. He ran the water over it to loosen the sludge, which he carefully picked out with a kitchen knife. As he began to free up the inside of the bell, he did not notice the dirt and water on the kitchen counter.

He was thinking of the impossible suggestion by his sister that it was from Santa's sleigh. The simple beauty of the bell became more apparent as it emerged from its dirt cocoon, and his imagination was brought to life when he considered the impossible being possible.

"Travis!" He was jolted back from his daydream by the voice of his mother. "What are you doing on the kitchen counter? Look at the dirt and...oh, what a mess!"

Susan was pretty, even when exasperated by the antics of her children. She had postponed a career in the advertising business in order to be a stay-at-home mom. She found it more challenging than any budget report had ever been and a hundred times more rewarding. Once both children were in school, she had begun part-time studies at the university towards a business degree.

"Look, Mom," explained Travis, "it's some sort of miniature bell. We found it in the leaves from the eavestroughs."

At this point Natalie piped in, "Yes, yes, and it's a sleigh bell from Santa's sleigh."

Before Susan could react either way, the children's father had reappeared to observe the scene.

"Young man, can't you be left alone for five minutes without creating some kind of disaster?" When he saw the knife in Travis' hand, his frustration and anger erupted as never before. "Have you lost your senses?" he roared. "That's the good paring knife, and you're using it to pick out dirt from some rusty old trinket!"

He was very protective of the kitchen knives. They had been a gift from his father, who was a chef, and they were respected and cared for at all times.

"But, Daddy, it's from Santa's sleigh and we found it!" proclaimed Natalie, sure that this explanation would justify any problem.

"I don't care whose bell it is, it doesn't mean you can do irresponsible things!"

Travis was stunned into silence. He was unprepared for the level of his father's anger.

"But, Dad..." he stammered.

"No 'But, Dad' this time, mister. Put that knife down...now. It's obvious to me that you aren't mature enough to handle such a potentially dangerous instrument. Now wipe that mess off the counter, and then it's up to your room for the rest of the evening."

"Ah, gee, I wanted to watch..."

"Another word and it'll be for the rest of the week."

There was silence among the family while Travis quickly cleaned the counter. As the kitchen radio softly played "It's Beginning to Look a Lot Like Christmas", Susan gently directed Natalie back to her colouring book and spent a few minutes admiring her younger child's efforts.

Travis was fighting back tears as he headed up to his room, where he almost made the error of slamming the door. However, common sense prevailed, and he quietly closed it. Sitting on the edge of his bed, he was surprised to look in his hand and see that he was still holding the small bell.

It had now become the sole cause of everything that had gone wrong, and he tossed it into his shoe box full of knick-knacks and assorted treasures, where it landed on an old baseball cap without making a sound.

Nobody slept very well that night, but they all made an extra effort with each other the next morning. Sunday breakfast was always a special meal, with everyone pitching in to help prepare it.

Travis was put in charge of setting the table, and

Natalie was concentrating on squeezing juice from the orange halves her father had cut for her. Susan made her specialty, a fresh fruit salad.

Jim had mixed the pancake batter earlier and was now adding the blueberries as he poured it onto the sizzling hot pan. He had taken the blueberries out of the freezer the night before, and they had reminded him of the hot August day when the whole family had driven north to the pine forest where their secret blueberry patch was thick with its delicious bounty.

He had shared those thoughts with Travis when, as usual, he had gone to say goodnight. Travis had brightened up at the memory of that summer day and, after apologizing to his father for his thoughtlessness with the knife, had drifted off to sleep.

Now they were sitting around the table sharing the week's experiences and enjoying each other's company. Natalie was preoccupied for most of the meal with the mint leaf floating in her orange juice. That is, until she spoke out, "Mommy, when are we decorating the house for Christmas? It's soon, you know."

"That's true, dear, and we should give it some thought," her mother replied. She had tried to discuss this very matter with Jim earlier in the week, but his concern over pending money problems had caused him to delay any discussion of the holiday season.

"Yeah, Mom, all my friends have their stuff up," added Travis, surprised at his own enthusiasm.

"And I have my letter to Santa all written. Do you have yours, Travis?" inquired Natalie.

Travis didn't know how to respond. He had become skeptical about the existence of Santa over the summer when some of the older boys at the baseball field had said a few negative things and teased the younger kids for their childish beliefs.

"We better send them soon. Right, Daddy?" continued Natalie.

"Look, kids," declared Jim, "we shouldn't get too worked up or excited about Christmas this year. You know I've been out of work for quite a while, and all the celebrating and presents can cost a lot of money..."

"Yes, but Santa will still come, even if you don't work...won't he?" pleaded Natalie.

"Of course he will, dear," interrupted Susan. "After all, you've been a very good girl this year...both of you have been good, so don't give it another thought. Your father was referring to the other aspects of the holiday. Isn't that right, honey?" She stared long and hard at Jim to be sure he got the message.

"That's right, Natalie. I didn't mean Santa wasn't coming," he reassured her.

"In fact," said Susan, "we'll mail those letters for you this afternoon, on the way to the Murray's party."

Jim squirmed in his chair at the mention of the party. He did not want to go to the open house and see all their friends and neighbours. He was embarrassed when people asked about his job and preferred to avoid talking with anyone. But he knew Susan wanted to go, so he would swallow his pride and try to have fun.

The rest of the meal went rather uneventfully, and after the clean-up, Natalie insisted that Travis get his letter to Santa written. He went along on the off-chance that those guys at the ballpark were wrong.

Later that afternoon, the whole family got bundled up and went for a walk down to the park by the lake. The skies were gray and cloudy, and the water's edge was crusted with a layer of ice as the temperature tumbled well below the freezing mark.

"Looks like we're in for a bit of snow," forecast Jim. "I can smell it in the air."

A puzzled Natalie sniffed and sniffed, but wasn't able to detect anything that would allow her to share her father's insight.

"I can hardly wait," said Susan. "There is always something special about the first snowfall. Everything gets a new coat of sparkling white, and it reminds me of all the good times I had when I was a child."

"Did you build forts and have snowball fights with your friends, Mom?" asked Travis.

"Oh, yes, and I had a pretty good throwing arm back then. Everyone wanted me on their side," she boasted.

"And did you make snowmen...and angels in the snow?" asked Natalie, excited by her mother's memories.

"Most definitely, honey. That's the great thing about snow and kids," explained Susan. "Each year you get to do the same things over again. The same things your mom and dad did when they were kids, and your grandparents did when they were kids, too. And even after all this time, it's still fun to do."

"And then," said Jim, "you get old enough to shovel it, scrape it, try to drive through it, and it's not as much fun anymore. In fact, it becomes a real pain in the..."

"Thank you, Mister Happy-Go-Lucky," interrupted Susan, shaking her head in frustration. "Come on everyone. We'd better head back. Your dad and I have to get dressed up for the party."

They took the shortcut home and pretended to have a snowball fight on the way. Natalie and her father claimed victory, although this was disputed by Susan and Travis, who predicted real victory when they got some genuine snow.

Back at home, the kids started watching an old Christmas movie on television. After a while, Jim and Susan emerged from their bedroom, dressed and ready for the party.

"Ta-dahhhhh...so, what do you think?" asked Susan, as she did her best runway model imitation across the family room floor.

"Oh, Mommy, you look beautiful!" replied Natalie.

Travis looked, smiled and gave a whistle of approval, followed by, "Wow!"

"Pretty nice looking, isn't she?" admired Jim. "Everyone at the party will be wondering what she's doing with a broken-down old guy like me."

"Daddy, you're not broken, just a little worn out, and I think you look very pretty too!" declared Natalie.

Travis howled with laughter. "Men aren't called pretty. They're supposed to be handsome."

"And that's exactly what your father is to me," proclaimed Susan.

"Thanks for those votes of confidence," chuckled Jim. "Okay, you kids know where we'll be. The Murray's phone number is on the message board, and we'll be home around six, so I'm trusting you'll both be on your best behaviour...or maybe we should call Louise to come and baby-sit."

"No way, Dad, we're not babies," said Travis. "We can take care of ourselves."

"All right then," replied Jim, as he buttoned his overcoat and opened the front door, "we'll see you later."

Susan kissed each of the children before heading out the door.

"Bye...have fun," called out the kids as the door closed. They turned their attention back to the television and watched the remainder of the movie.

As the closing credits were rolling, Natalie was struck by an idea that she hoped her brother would agree with.

"Travis, why don't we surprise Mom and Dad and get out the Christmas decorations? Then when they get back from the party, all the work will be done and it will be Christmassy."

He thought for a moment, and not being able to come up with anything else to do and hoping to find a way to make up for the previous night's misdeed, he nodded in agreement. "Okay, little sister, that's a neat idea! Mom and Dad will be gone for three hours, so that should give us loads of time. Let's do it!"

"Yippee, it's time for Christmas at the Kirkland house!" cried out Natalie. "Come on, let's get the boxes out of the storage room."

"Hold on. Dad always starts with Christmas music to help get in the mood first," said Travis, as he opened the stereo cabinet and searched through the cassette rack. "Here it is...*Christmas Music - New and Old* ."

It was a tape their father had made of his favourite Christmas songs, and the kids knew all the words and music. Their voices joined in, loud and joyful, as they carried up the fifteen boxes of decorations from the basement. A couple were heavy enough that it took both children to lift them up the stairs and onto the main floor.

They were having so much fun that they didn't even notice it was beginning to snow. It was only after the last box was placed in the kitchen that Natalie glanced through the sliding glass doors and became aware of the dusting of white that was gently falling to the ground.

"Travis," she yelled, running to press her face against the glass, "it's snowing, it's snowing! We're going to have a white Christmas, just like the song says!" She began to sing the most famous Christmas song.

Travis came over to the window and grinned as he saw the dull brown colours of the back yard disappearing in a sea of white. He hummed along to his sister's vocalizing as they both stood and watched the magical transformation.

After a couple of minutes, Travis instructed Natalie to open the box of stuffed toys in the family room and start placing them around.

He headed for the living room to tackle the ceramic village of Dickens figures that the family had been collecting since he was a baby. He had helped his dad set up the display for the last couple of years and felt confident he could accomplish the task on his own. After a little while, Natalie came in.

"The stuffed toys are all out. What can I do next?" she asked.

"Um-m-m, how about the candles in the box on the kitchen floor," Travis replied. "Get them all out and put them on top of the table. I should be ready to help display them by then."

He didn't realize how long it was going to take to

carefully unpack and unwrap each figurine, and he wasn't even halfway through when Natalie returned.

"The candles are all out. Come on and help," she said.

"Uh-h-h, gee, this is taking longer...how about you unpack the front hall decorations. Just put them on the floor to start with," answered Travis.

He was surrounded by a pile of tissue wrapping paper, which grew bigger with each ceremonious un-wrapping. He might have accomplished his task faster if he had not spent a few minutes studying each figure up close and recalling its little biography.

"Hey, Travis," yelled Natalie from the front hall, "the music has stopped. Can I put on another tape?"

"Okay. Anything but the singing turtle one; it's for babies," he replied as Natalie ran to the stereo.

"Oh yeah, that's just for little kids," she agreed out loud, while telling herself she would listen to it another time when he wasn't around. She picked out *Mitch Miller and the Gang Holiday Sing-along* so that she could test herself on "The Twelve Days of Christmas".

As she made her way back to the front hall, she was loudly accompanying the recording, and even Travis could not resist a forceful harmony when it reached "five golden rings". They were both brim-ming with Christmas cheer as they continued their decorating tasks.

"Hey, Jim-bo! Season's greetings, pal. How ya' been?"

The only thing Jim disliked more than being called 'Jim-bo' was being called 'pal'. These terms made him cringe when they were directed at him.

But what made it even worse was that this was coming from Ken Corrigan. He was a long-time employee of the same company that had let Jim go. Not a loyal or even honest employee, but a rather devious one.

Jim had managed to avoid him for most of the afternoon, but it wasn't a big party and now their paths were crossing.

"Very well, Ken, and a Merry Christmas to you," replied Jim, hoping that would be the end of the discussion.

Ken, however, had been partying to excess, as usual, and he wasn't about to let his former colleague escape his attention so easily.

"Say, guy," he inquired, "any luck on the job market?" It was loud enough so that anyone at the party who hadn't known, knew now.

"No, nothing yet. I'm still looking for the right opportunity," Jim replied, turning towards the buffet table.

"Ah, that's a shame," continued Ken, with a slight

smugness in his tone. He had been very threatened by Jim's presence at the company and had taken every opportunity to undermine Jim's position, especially after the new owners had taken over. "It's really rough out there these days. I've had to burn the midnight oil to keep my sales figures ahead of budget."

He lied, of course. This was a man who never showed up before 8:30 a.m., never worked through lunch and never stayed five minutes longer than his superiors at the end of the day.

It was at moments like this that Jim was overcome with feelings of doubt and guilt about the decisions he had made regarding his work.

Two years earlier, he had left a stressful job, which paid very well but required lots of travelling away from home. He accepted a lower paying position in a large corporation in order to spend more time with his family. But the company was sold within a year, and the new owners had cut back the number of employees in all departments. He was among the last to go.

Jim and Susan assumed it wouldn't take long for him to find another job, since he was in his prime, with a good education and solid experience.

Unfortunately, thousands of other people were in the same circumstances, as many companies were making similar cut-backs. Timing, as the saying goes, is everything, and his timing had been terrible.

"Sorry to break up this little reunion, fellows, but I

need Jim's help in the kitchen," interrupted their host.

Ian Murray was a good friend to Jim, and they enjoyed getting together and exchanging philosophies of marriage, fatherhood and lifestyles, while catching a few fish or tending the barbecue. He had seen Jim being harassed by their fellow neighbour and had come to the rescue.

"Ah, the things we have to do in the name of maintaining the holiday spirit."

"Thanks, Ian," said Jim, as they entered the kitchen. "I was about to lose my good manners with that blowhard. He's got the nerve to claim his hard work is responsible for their good sales figures. Funny how he forgets to mention that his main competition has had a labour disruption for five months."

"Hey, don't let him get to you. He's not worth the aggravation."

"Yeah, I know. It's just that I'm getting more nervous about everything these days."

"Well, that's understandable, but you've got to stay positive. Something will come up, and in the meantime," chuckled Ian, "keep buying those lottery tickets."

He always knew how to get a laugh out of Jim. They both smiled and recalled their fall fishing trip, when they had daydreamed of sharing a big jackpot if they ever did win.

Travis realized he was in over his head as he surveyed the situation around him. All the ceramic figures and their accompanying accessories were now unwrapped and ready to be positioned. Unfortunately, he had failed to remember all the electrical wiring and taping down of cords that had to be done before the village could be assembled. He tried a couple of approaches, but the complexity of the display was somewhat overwhelming. Yet, it had been done before, and he certainly wasn't going to give up.

However, for now, he needed a break, so he went to the kitchen to satisfy a seasonal craving.

"Hey, Natalie, how about an eggnog?" he called out.

"No thanks," she grimaced, not yet having developed a taste for the rich, creamy beverage.

"Doesn't matter, there isn't any," said Travis, staring into the refrigerator. "Want a hot chocolate with marshmallows?"

"That's more like it," said Natalie, "especially if you add a little *cimanon*, like Mom does."

"You got it, sis!" he said, chuckling at her mispronunciation of cinnamon.

He carefully poured the milk into each mug and then added heaping tablespoons of chocolate syrup, stirring vigorously as he thought of the delicious glob of chocolate that would be resting at the bottom of his cup. He popped them into the microwave oven for a couple of minutes and rummaged through the pantry for the marshmallows and cinnamon powder. A quick stir, enough miniature marshmallows to cover the top, followed by a dash of cinnamon, and the drinks were ready. He carefully carried them out to the front hall where Natalie was occupied stringing the artificial pine boughs around the staircase banister.

"Here you go, Nat," he said, handing her the warm cup.

She mumbled a quick thanks as she plunged her face into the softened marshmallows.

"M-m-m-m, delicious," she exclaimed. "So, what do you think?" She was referring to her decorating.

He didn't want to dampen her enthusiasm, so he diplomatically replied, "Well, you've certainly found a place for everything in the boxes. Of course, Mom may want to do some fine tuning, but you've definitely got things started."

Every shelf, corner, stair, doorknob and wall had something hanging, sitting or leaning on it.

"Here, let me show you another way to wrap the pine boughs on the banister." He put his cup on the front hall table, and she carefully placed hers on the floor by the front door. "If you thread it through each spindle, it's too much like a spring. What you need to do is skip every three spindles so it has more of a hanging effect." This was how his mother had shown him a few years ago when he had made the same error as Natalie.

"Oh, now I get it. Yeah, it does look better. Let me try the rest."

Together they connected, wove and adjusted the boughs all the way up the staircase and into the upstairs hall, unaware of how much time had passed since they began their efforts to get the Christmas season off to a glorious start.

The party at the Murray's got livelier throughout the afternoon, especially when they noticed the snow. It was as if they were all kids again. The Christmas music was turned up louder, and they recalled humorous stories of snow-related incidents from the past. They even had a traditional sing-along around the piano with Jim chording some of the more popular tunes.

Everyone was having a great time, and it was past 6:00 p.m. before people reluctantly remembered they had Sunday dinners and kids to get home to. Sincere thanks, good-byes and heartfelt Christmas wishes were extended by everyone.

Of course, Ken was slurring his way through the niceties but still managed another verbal jab at Jim while stumbling out the door.

"Say, Jimmy boy, you have yourself a great tinsel time, an' an even better New Year. Give me a call sometime, an' you can take me out to lunch. I'll give you some good advice."

It may have been the fifth drink or the fact that he hadn't worn overshoes and the snow was now quite deep. Whatever the cause, Ken lost his balance and what little dignity he had, with a slip and a fall that landed him flat on his back in the street. The departing neighbours stifled their chuckles as Mrs. Corrigan scolded her impaired husband and marched off down the road with him in limping pursuit.

Jim and Susan warmly thanked Ian and his wife, Michelle, and made tentative plans to get together with the kids on Christmas Eve.

As they carefully walked arm in arm down the street, Jim's party mood was chilled by the cold and thoughts of Ken Corrigan. Susan noticed the change but said nothing, relieved that, at least for part of the afternoon, the old Jim had returned.

His hearty laugh and off-key singing had been proof of that, and she would encourage these loved characteristics to appear more often.

They were each lost in their own thoughts as they turned onto their front walk. The silence of the evening was courtesy of the large, soft snowflakes that drifted slowly to earth, filtering out the sounds that normally filled the air.

The calm was broken only by the jingling of Jim's key ring as he searched for the correct key and then inserted it into the front door lock. He quickly turned it to the left, then squeezed the door latch and briskly pushed open the door. The resulting collision with the almost full cup of hot chocolate sitting on the entrance hall floor startled everyone.

Travis and Natalie had just finished the pine boughs and were sitting on the staircase overlooking the scene around them. Their momentary feeling of pride had been interrupted by the clicking of the lock, which immediately drew Travis' gaze towards the front door.

At that exact moment, he saw Natalie's cup on the floor and began to leap from his place. Too late! The door flew open, smashing the cup. Chocolate milk and melted marshmallow were sent flying in all directions. Travis froze in his steps, his eyes staring at the hot chocolate that dripped everywhere.

Natalie's jaw dropped like Marley's ghost's.

Jim and Susan stood in the open doorway, aghast at the sight before them. The mish-mash of Christmas decorations, crumpled packing papers and empty boxes alone would have been enough to shock them. But the sound created by the breaking cup and the liquid aftermath was the straw that broke the camel's back for Jim. As he stepped around the brown puddles, he finally saw the children on the stairs.

"For crying out loud, what have you two been up to now?" he demanded.

Both Travis and Natalie were silent as they desperately tried to find words to explain the situation. Jim peered across the living room and saw the unfinished Christmas decorating spread through the whole house.

Susan had now eased her way into the hall and expressed her dismay. "Oh, kids, I really wish you had checked with me before dragging all this stuff out."

Natalie tried to say something, but her emotions got the best of her. She remained silent as large tears began a slow descent down her quivering cheeks. Travis came down the stairs and began his explanation.

"Gosh, Mom, we just wanted to help out and surprise you." His voice faded out as he felt the harsh gaze of his father.

"Well, don't just stand there, get a bucket of warm water and some old towels to mop up this...this...what is this?"

Natalie moaned as she identified the liquid. "It's hot chocolate. Travis made some to help get us into the Christmas spirit while we decorated. Just like you used to do, Daddy, when you liked Christmas."

Even through his anger, Jim was startled by his daughter's statement and momentarily hesitated in his reaction. Travis used this opportunity to deflect any more of his father's outburst away from Natalie.

"That was my cup...I guess I must have put it down by the door. I didn't think you'd be home so soon."

"Well, you got the 'didn't think' part right. Now get the towels and clean it up."

Susan had seen the quizzical reaction on Natalie's face as Travis gave his explanation, and she guessed his confession was an act of brotherly protectiveness. Closing the door behind her, she removed her coat and put it in the closet. She then went over to console Natalie who had now stopped crying.

"You did a great job with the pine boughs on the banister, honey."

"Travis showed me the right way to do it, Mommy." she sobbed.

"Well, you're pretty lucky to have a brother who's as nice as he is."

Jim had wandered over to the bay window where the Dickens' Village was unpacked and ready for assembly. He thought about the first couple of Christmases when Travis was a baby and they had started collecting the figurines. It was now so complicated that Jim had taken notes when he'd dismantled it last year, in hopes of making the task of setting it up a little easier. Travis hadn't stood a chance, but his effort was commendable.

"Come on, son, let's get this chocolate cleaned up before anything gets stained."

Travis lugged the bucket of water and some towels

into the front hall and proceeded to mop up. Natalie was quick to join in and help her brother.

In the background Mitch Miller and the Gang cheerily sang "Winter Wonderland", and both Jim and Susan found themselves humming along as they joined in the clean-up. This seemed to calm what was a tense situation, and when Jim spoke again his tone was firm, but controlled.

"When this is finished, I want you both to go to your rooms until dinner is ready. Your mother and I are going to have to discuss how to handle this situation. Especially your ongoing lack of responsibility, Travis. At this point, I am very disappointed in you."

Nobody said a word in response as they wiped the last of the chocolate milk off the wall and swept up the remains of the cup.

"Okay, off you go," said Susan. "I'll call you when it's time to come down."

Both children slowly climbed the stairs as Jim headed into the kitchen to begin preparing dinner. He realized the kids had only been trying to enjoy what had always been the best time of the year.

Christmas is special, especially for young children. Their openness to the magic of the holiday season will never be as great as at this time of their lives. Some will be lucky and carry part of it with them into adulthood, while for others this will be the only time when they can appreciate the joy and love that are the underlying emotions of the Yuletide spirit. Together with the laughter that occurs among families, friends and even strangers, this magic creates bonds that link generations.

Jim knew this and believed it with all his heart. So, as he peeled the potatoes, he decided that it was time to put aside his concerns temporarily and do everything in his power to ensure that this would be another great Christmas for the whole family.

Susan was making her way slowly towards the kitchen. The afternoon's party had definitely put her into the Christmas spirit. The sight of all their family treasures - which she considered much more than decorations - was strengthening that emotion with each step...the pop bottle covered in papier-mache and sculpted to look like St. Nicholas that Travis had made in grade two art class...the hand-blown glass tree ornaments that had hung on her grandparents' and parents' Christmas trees...the old music box that Jim had purchased at an estate auction and then spent countless hours reconditioning, so that its delicate rendition of "Have Yourself a Merry Little Christmas" could again delight its listeners...and the handcrafted snowflakes that Natalie had so proudly made only last year.

These and all the rest of the items brought back wonderful memories from all the Christmases she had known.

Now, as she entered the kitchen, she was determined to get her husband's attention off the spilled milk and onto the task of preparing for Christmas.

"You know, Jim, you were wrong with your accusation of lack of responsibility against Travis. On the contrary, he took full responsibility for getting out the decorations and trying to get this family into the Christmas spirit, which it is so sadly lacking this year. And I also suspect he went a few steps further and took responsibility for the mug of hot chocolate on the floor that most likely was placed there by Natalie."

"Now, if that doesn't demonstrate the kind of ideals that we hope to be teaching our children, then I think you and I need to be discussing our actions and not the kids'. It's a few days before Christmas, and we are way behind in celebrating what has always been our favourite time. We may not have a lot to celebrate during the rest of the year, but Christmas has always enjoyed an immunity from the problems of the other eleven months. I believe we are wrong for not maintaining that special feeling."

She paused long enough for Jim to speak up.

"You are, as usual, absolutely right," he replied. "And if you agree, I think we should get the rest of the decorations unpacked and displayed, as soon as we've cleaned up after dinner."

Susan was caught slightly off guard by Jim's response, but she quickly approached him and gave him a big kiss on the lips, softly commenting, "Now, that's more like the man I fell in love with."

He dried his hands on his apron towel and then embraced his wife. "You know, sometimes I can act like a bit of a jerk."

"Oh yes, believe me, I know," she responded. "But you're my jerk."

They kissed again, then set about getting dinner ready.

Travis sat on the edge of his bed, bewildered by what had happened. It seemed that lately, no matter what he did, it ended up with him getting into trouble. It might have been easier to accept if he was a bad child, which he wasn't. So then, why did everything keep backfiring on him?

It was very confusing and filled him with self-doubt. In no time at all he had worked himself into quite a state. His emotions had gotten the best of him, and he really wasn't thinking clearly.

Travis was convinced that his parents didn't love or trust him, and it would just serve them right if he ran away.

Of course, he didn't know where he'd go or what he'd do, but to this 10-year-old boy, the decision to pack a bag and leave home made, for the moment, perfect sense.

He opened his closet door and pulled out his nylon knapsack. It would be ideal for carrying the bare essentials that he would need. He took out two pairs of underwear and t-shirts and three pairs of heavy socks. He included his favourite wool sweater, because it might come in handy, this being December and all. He thought of going to get his toothbrush from the bathroom but, in a display of rebellion, decided dental hygiene would not have any place in the new life he was embarking on. With each article he packed, his confidence in this adventure grew more intense. A turtleneck completed his clothing requirements.

"Boy, this is going to show them," he thought to himself. "I'm never getting sent to my room again."

His feeling of determination was growing as he picked through his shoe box. There was the envelope containing the ten-dollar bill he'd received from his Uncle Brian on his last birthday, and the five-dollar bill he'd found wedged in a bush while searching for a lost ball. He was saving the money for Christmas gifts, but that wasn't going to be necessary anymore. He took out a pocket knife and mini-flashlight and even found 48 cents in change, which certainly would be useful. A half pack of sugarless gum, especially since he was no longer brushing his teeth, completed his packing.

It was then that he saw the tiny bell that he'd tossed into the box the night before. He picked it up and looked closely at it, marvelling at how detailed the etching was. He rubbed it on his sleeve to buff the shine a little, then placed it in his palm and remarked, "Geez, for something so small, you sure did cause a lot of trouble."

He then held it by the leather strap and shook it. It rang with such a pure sound that it startled him, and he stopped. He looked closer as if trying to x-ray the inside and then shook it a second time. Again, the sound came forth. It was both familiar and yet completely mysterious, quite unlike any bell he'd heard before. He was so captivated that he rang it for a third time.

As he listened to the purity of the sound, he suddenly realized all this bell ringing might attract some attention, so he quickly placed it in his knapsack, tightened the drawstring and buckled the flap.

He took one quick look around his room, slipped out into the hallway and passed the closed door of Natalie's room. He paused when he heard her singing "Jingle Bells" and wondered if she'd heard the bell. It was probably just a coincidence, but he didn't stop to find out.

He carefully tiptoed down the stairs and over to the front hall closet, taking out his boots and pulling them on. He donned his scarf and hat before quietly zipping up his winter coat. He didn't look back into the house, fearful he might have second thoughts. Instead, he opened the door, stepped into the snow on the front porch, and silently pulled the door closed.

"Christmas," he mumbled dejectedly, "yeah, I guess it is just for little kids."

He hoisted the full knapsack onto his shoulder and put on his mitts as he walked down the pathway, disappearing into the oncoming snowfall.

CHAPTER TWO

Snowstorms
and
Sleighrides

t the sound of the first ringing of the bell, Ogilthorpe stopped what he was doing, held his breath, and cocked his tiny head to one side. The only other sound was heavy breathing by the other occupant of the stall.

"Quiet, Dasher," he instructed.

The second ringing made his eyes grow big.

"That's it!" he exclaimed. "Come on, now. One more time." His anticipation was almost electric. And when the third and most important ringing of the bell occurred, it was as if someone had thrown a switch and illuminated a three-storey-tall Christmas tree.

"Ya-hoo! It's the bell. Oh, Dasher, I woke up this morning and just knew it was going to be a great day, but I never thought it would be this great."

Even though he hadn't heard anything and Ogilthorpe had stopped giving him his daily brushing, the majestic creature was so pleased his little friend was this happy that he let out a yelp of excitement to acknowledge his good feelings too, "Ah-h ro-o-o!"

That's just the way it's always been at the North

Pole. Everyone has a good time and loves to share good feelings with everyone else. Happiness is everywhere, from Santa himself down to the tiniest chipmunk that lives in the evergreen forest encircling the village.

And what a village it is! There is always some activity going on, not because it's demanded, but because every task, every chore and responsibility is undertaken with a sense of fun and enjoyment.

For that is their purpose — to enjoy what they do so much that they want to keep doing it. That's the way it has been since anyone can remember.

Ogilthorpe, like all the other elves, had certainly encountered his share of problems over the years. Take the time the Candy Factory was experiencing trouble with the new peppermint flavour. It was coming out too spicy, so as the elf in charge, he worked day and night for two months to come up with the perfect formula. In the end, everyone said it was the best flavour they had ever tasted, and it's stayed that way for the last hundred years.

So, when he had discovered the bell was missing, he'd made double sure that the other bells were all secure and that each reindeer's harness was well cleaned and oiled.

But he never forgot about the missing bell.

"Great peppermint snowflakes, I almost thought I'd seen the last of that bell. It could have fallen into the ocean and been swallowed by a giant oyster or perhaps gotten wedged in the branches of a mighty redwood along the coastal rain forest."

Ogilthorpe's mind was racing through all the different possibilities he had imagined ever since he'd realized the bell was missing. That was almost a year ago when the sleigh had returned from the big trip last Christmas.

Now, it wasn't unusual for a bell to go missing. It had happened...two or three times in the last couple of hundred years. Ogilthorpe, however, didn't want a missing bell occurrence during his tour of duty as Stablemaster, and so he had not told anyone about it. He had a feeling that sometime, somehow, he would find the bell.

There was a renewed vigour in his brushing of Dasher's fur as he explained the situation to the antlered beast.

"You see, my friend, last year after the big trip, when I was cleaning and storing all the special-occasion harnesses, I noticed the last bell on the chest strap of your harness was gone. It seems the leather had cracked and ripped apart. It must have been loose to start with. Unless you bumped into a chimney or some tree tops?"

Dasher shook his head, and Ogilthorpe chuckled at his little joke.

"No, no, I realize I must have missed the cracks

during my preflight check. So it was my fault and, therefore, it is my responsibility to get it back. It's a good thing these pointy ears of mine are specially tuned to the ringing of the magic sleigh bells. The first ring gets your attention...the second ring allows you to be sure it's one of the magic bells...the third and most important ring allows you to pinpoint its location, with the help of one of Santa's Magic Snowballs. Now, if I plan this properly, we should be able to get the bell back and not have to bother anybody else. You will help me, Dasher, won't you?"

Dasher eagerly nodded his head and pawed at the floor in anticipation of the adventure.

Ogilthorpe always brushed Dasher last and spent a little longer with him than with the other reindeer. They had developed a special friendship and often liked to go sledding through the forest trails late in the evening, when only the moon and stars shone down on the sparkling white landscape. While they glided cheerfully over hills and through valleys, Ogilthorpe would sing his favourite Christmas songs.

Occasionally, Dasher would practise takeoffs and landings just to keep in tiptop form for the yearly trip down south, although Ogilthorpe much preferred it when they stayed in contact with the ground.

"BONG, BONG, BONG."

It was the courtyard bell signaling everyone to stop working and get cleaned up for dinner.

"Okay, pal, I've got to go now, but I'll be back after dinner, and we'll head out." Dasher nodded, then stepped over to the feed bin and began eating, for he knew it was important to have a nutritious meal before going on a long flight.

Ogilthorpe closed the stall door, headed out of the reindeer stable and into the courtyard. He smiled at the sight of happy elves heading in all directions. Out of the Candy Factory, from the Toy Shoppe, whistling, singing, laughing. It was a glorious sight.

"Good evening, Ogilthorpe. How are the reindeer doing? All ready for the big trip?"

"Oh yes, Cornelius, they are in top form and very excited," replied Ogilthorpe. "How are things at the bakery?"

Cornelius paused, sniffed the air, and his upturned nose twitched. "Hm-m-m, the shortbreads just came out of the oven, and the gingerbreads will be ready in about five minutes. We'll be having some for dessert tonight...a special treat! I must hurry back now. Have a nice evening!"

"You too. Bye-bye," said Ogilthorpe, making a mental note to pack a couple of extra cookies to munch on during the trip to retrieve the bell.

It always takes a while to get anywhere in Santa's Village because everybody is so friendly and always interested in what everyone else is doing. Especially at this time of year, when all the efforts of the past twelve months come together and culminate with Santa's trip.

The elves were feeling wonderful tonight, and when a few of them from the Games and Trains Shoppe started singing "Santa Claus Is Coming to Town", it only took a few notes before the whole village was joining in and bursting with song. The harmonies were intricately woven, and each elf knew his part.

Singing is second nature to elves. During the year, they practise and practise so that moments like this can happen. At the end of the song, they gleefully applauded themselves and continued on their way.

Inside the huge bunkhouse, Ogilthorpe carefully hung up his overalls and changed into his evening clothes, but not before putting on his extra thick long underwear. He had decided to head out while everyone else was having dinner.

First, he would visit Santa's Workshop, where the jolly old fellow works on new ideas for children's toys and keeps the list of good boys and girls. Ogilthorpe had finished a rotation as an assistant in Santa's Workshop before becoming Stablemaster a few years ago.

He knew exactly what he needed, and that was one of Santa's Magic Snowballs. They are used to 'see' the children when they are sleeping or awake, helping to determine if they will be put on the list of good children.

All Ogilthorpe needed to do was vibrate his ears to

the exact same frequency as the missing bell, and a picture of it would appear in the Magic Snowball, showing where the bell was when it had been rung. Then he and Dasher would fly out and get it back. It seemed pretty straightforward to Ogilthorpe. He even figured he could reattach the bell to Dasher's harness before going to bed. It would be a long evening, but well worth the effort.

He quickly pulled on his coat and headed into the dining hall. He may have to miss dinner, but he wasn't going to forget Cornelius' gingerbread cookies, which were in a jar at the end of the buffet table. He wrapped a couple in a napkin and placed them in his inside coat pocket. They smelled delicious and were still warm, which felt good as he headed back outside.

"Say, Ogilthorpe, are you finished your dinner already?" asked Dudley. He had been a good friend since they had apprenticed together in the Doll Shoppe a long time ago.

"Why, hello, Dudley. I'm just off to do a couple of errands. My, my, you look like you've already had your dinner," said Ogilthorpe, gently patting the bulging tummy of his rotund friend.

"Oh dear, it's all that special baking of Cornelius'. I just can't help myself. In fact, I'm thinking about gingerbread cookies right now as we stand here."

Ogilthorpe smiled at the thought of the delicious cookies in his pocket. "Then you better hurry inside because tonight is your lucky night." They laughed, shook hands, and headed in different directions...Dudley to the dining hall and Ogilthorpe towards Santa's Workshop.

The snow crunched under Ogilthorpe's boots as he walked across the courtyard to the stone and log structure that always gave him a special feeling.

It had been the first of all the buildings in Santa's Village. Even though other, bigger facilities had been built over the years, it still was considered the centre of operations. All the elves looked forward to a tour of duty here because it meant a little extra time with Santa himself, who, while always busy, still managed to inject a sense of fun and pride into what they were accomplishing together.

The heavy, carved door creaked as Ogilthorpe pushed it open. It seemed so strange that the only noise was the crackling of embers in the massive stone fireplace. It wouldn't be like that for long. As soon as the elves had finished dinner and had sung a few Christmas songs, they would be heading back to their work stations to get caught up with the backlog that always occurs just before Christmas.

Ogilthorpe crossed the room and pulled himself onto the tall stool at the high desk. He opened the side window, and there on the ledge was one of Santa's Magic Snowballs.

No one really knows how they work, but like so

many things in the village, it is an accepted part of Christmas magic. And, as Santa often says, it only works for those who believe.

Now, instead of a Magic Snowball, Ogilthorpe could have used Santa's special telescope. From high up at the North Pole it is possible to see down over all the world. But he did not have time to climb all the stairs to a lookout window. It was faster and easier to use a Magic Snowball.

Ogilthorpe stared at the large sphere and concentrated so hard that the tips of his pointy elf ears began to vibrate. Slowly at first, then increasing in speed as they emitted a pure, rich tone. It started very low, but the pitch rose as the vibrations went faster, until the sound matched exactly the frequency that had been attained when the bell was rung three times.

All at once, the snowball on the ledge began to glow, and soon it was crystal clear. Inside it was the image of Travis in his bedroom. Ogilthorpe leaned closer and focussed his eyes as he wanted to be absolutely sure.

"Hm-m-m, that looks a lot like...yes...I believe that's Travis Kirkland. My, my, he's getting bigger every year."

The image was blurry, and this saddened Ogilthorpe.

"Oh dear, don't fade away." He knew this meant only one thing. Travis was beginning to lose his faith in the magic of Christmas, and there was nothing

Ogilthorpe or anyone could do to stop it.

Then the image disappeared, and the snowball stopped glowing.

"Well, let's check the incoming letters to Santa." He turned the stool around to the desk and opened the incoming letter ledger for that year, but there was nothing from Travis, which was another bad sign.

Still, the image hadn't been completely blurry and mail was arriving every day, so perhaps things weren't as bleak as they seemed. At least now he knew where the bell was, and in no time at all he and Dasher would recover it.

Ogilthorpe closed the ledger, shut the window and hopped down from the stool. He quickly made his way to the door, pausing only to take a candy cane from the silver bowl on the table.

"M-m-m-m, peppermint. My favourite," he said proudly as he stepped back outside and made his way over to the Reindeer Stable.

All the other reindeer were asleep in their stalls, resting up from a busy day of pre-flight exercises. Only Dasher was awake and standing as Ogilthorpe came into the stable.

"Good evening, Dasher. Are you all ready for the trip?" he whispered.

Dasher nodded excitedly.

"Come on then, we'll harness up out back by the training sleigh."

They quietly went outside, and in a few minutes
Dasher was harnessed and attached to the sleigh.
Ogilthorpe was a little nervous as he instructed his
friend.

"Now be careful on the takeoffs and landings and
watch out for flocks of Canada geese. You know I'm
a little uneasy about flying, so please don't go any
higher than necessary."

Dasher nodded confidently, and this calmed
Ogilthorpe as he stepped into the sleigh.

"Okay, Dasher, next stop...the home of Travis
Kirkland."

The sleigh lurched forward while Dasher gained
momentum, and then in a few steps the reindeer leapt
from the ground, pulling the sleigh and Ogilthorpe
silently into the night sky.

The Kirkland's kitchen was warm with the scent of
another delicious meal. Jim was quite a good chef,
thanks to his father, and as a way of getting his new
Christmas outlook across to the children, he had spent
an extra twenty minutes doing some intricate carvings
in the mushroom caps and vegetables. The kids
always liked the designs and shapes he made.

"Okay, Susan," he said, "everything's about ready

to go. If you'll tell the kids to wash up and come down, I'll start putting the food out."

As she got up from the kitchen table, where she had been sorting the large selection of Christmas candles, she commented, "Smells like another great meal. I'll just turn up the Christmas music before getting the kids."

"Great idea," he replied. "You read my mind."

They smiled at each other, for this was a feeling they often had. The years together had given them a sixth sense about each other, and it was comforting to know they were still in sync.

After resetting the tape machine and increasing the volume, Susan headed up the stairs to get the children. She knocked on Natalie's door, then pushed it open.

"Dinner's ready, honey," she said. "Wash your hands and come downstairs."

"Are you guys still mad at us?" asked Natalie. She had been giving the situation a lot of thought as she drew more Christmas pictures to decorate her room. "Because, you know, it was...it was my cup on the floor. I'm very sorry."

"That's okay, Natalie. I sort of thought it may have been yours. It was just a big shock to come home and see everything unpacked. The chocolate milk was only an accident. We all have accidents." She hugged her daughter, then kissed her on the forehead. "Come on, now. Dad's cooked a special dinner, and I think we've got a nice surprise for everyone."

Natalie smiled and jumped off her bed, running to the bathroom to wash up. Susan went to Travis' room and knocked.

"Travis, may I come in?" she asked. She had stopped entering without permission a few months ago as her son began asserting his rights of privacy as a pre-teen. "Travis, I'd like to talk with you." Still no response. "Honey, your dad and I are sorry we overreacted before. We want to get Christmas started properly, and your dad has made a special meal to help kick things off."

Still nothing. She knocked again.

"Travis, I'm coming in." She slowly eased the door open and stepped into the room. As she was about to start speaking, she looked around and realized he wasn't at his desk or on his bed.

"Travis?" she queried, glancing behind the door. "Travis, enough fooling around."

More silence.

Susan opened his closet, half expecting him to jump out, but it contained only clothes and shoes. She knelt down and checked under the bed, then called out loudly, "Travis!"

Natalie appeared at the door with a quizzical look on her face. "What's wrong, Mommy?"

"Have you seen Travis?"

"Not since we came upstairs. Maybe he went back down to the basement."

"Will you run downstairs and check please and, if he's there, tell him to come up and get washed for dinner."

"Okay, Mommy," replied Natalie as she bounded down the stairs.

Susan noticed that Travis' shoe box of knick-knacks had been emptied onto the bed. She left his room and headed downstairs. She was coming through the front hall when Natalie ran up to her.

"He's not in the basement, Mommy. I even looked behind the furnace!"

"Thanks, Natalie." Now Susan was getting worried. She hesitated as she walked over to the closet, then opened the door and looked at the coats. Not seeing Travis', she glanced down to where his boots should have been and saw an empty space.

She could feel the knot in her stomach tightening, and she wished she had gotten the children sooner, instead of waiting for dinner to be prepared.

"Did Travis go somewhere, Mommy?" asked Natalie.

"I don't know, sweetie. Come on, let's go to the kitchen."

She took her by the hand and briskly walked through the living room and into the kitchen.

"So who's in the mood for a little something special tonight?" asked Jim, with a big smile on his face.

"Travis went outside, Daddy," blurted Natalie.

Susan's and Jim's eyes met, and he immediately saw the concern in hers.

"Natalie, go get that picture of the Christmas tree you drew to show your daddy," said Susan, so she could talk to Jim.

As soon as their daughter left, Susan said, "He wasn't in his room or anywhere else. And his coat and boots are gone from the closet."

Jim put down the wooden spoon and leaned on the counter. Shaking his head, he sighed, "Darn, I should have talked to him earlier. Well, he certainly won't go very far at this hour. Let me put the food in the oven to stay warm, and I'll get the car to go look for him."

"I'll take care of the food," said Susan. "You get dressed and start looking."

She didn't want to waste any time having this situation attended to. Nodding, Jim removed his apron and swung open the kitchen door.

Natalie reappeared, proudly exclaiming, "See, Daddy, it's my best one yet."

He glanced at the artwork, then excused himself, "That's fantastic, Natalie. I'll sit down with it a little later, but right now I've got an errand I have to do."

"Come here, Natalie," said Susan, "I need some help in the kitchen."

Jim quickly put on his coat, boots and hat. He

grabbed the car keys off the hook and opened the front door. The blast of cold arctic air startled him as he noticed the intensity of the snowfall. Part of him was relieved, because he thought the dismal weather would encourage an early end to their runaway's adventurous mood. However, another part of him was deeply concerned as he drove off in search of his son.

Travis had gone several blocks before he realized he hadn't planned exactly where he would go or what he would do. Already the snow was coming down harder, and he considered turning back as his stomach growled and he thought of the nice warm meal he was missing. But his stubborn pride wouldn't let him. After all, he reasoned, what's the use in running away if you go back before they even know you're gone?

He then thought of the old lean-to he and his best friend, Andy Murray, had discovered in the ravine beside the park last summer. It had been run down and neglected, but they'd spent several days fixing it up with branches and stones until it became the base camp fort for many hours of make-believe adventures. At least there he could get out of the storm for a while and rethink his plan.

The snow and wind were now so strong that he

was having difficulty seeing the houses from the sidewalk, and he increased his pace to reach his destination sooner. He was glad he had packed the wool sweater. Putting it on would be the first thing he would do at the fort. He tried to look at his watch, but the cold wind was making his eyes water so much he could not focus.

He didn't notice a car coming up the street until it was almost beside him. It slowed momentarily, then continued down the road, its solitary occupant carefully studying the situation.

Travis thought for sure the street to take for the park would be coming up soon. He had no idea that he had passed it ten minutes ago and was now several blocks beyond where he wanted to be or where it was safe to be. He hesitantly started across the road, realizing he had to inch his foot along just to find the curb. At this point he was having second thoughts about his actions and was realizing it was probably best to head home. The wind was now a deafening howl, and the snow flew with such force that it stung his cheeks on contact.

The car's headlights were suddenly upon him, and Travis stood frozen in their path. It swerved to avoid hitting him, then continued into the storm, the taillights disappearing in a wall of white.

Travis was now completely lost. He didn't know which way the street went or where the curbs were.

He didn't know when another car might come barreling down on him, and the next time it might not miss.

A gloved hand suddenly landed on his shoulder.

"Hey, kid!" a voice rasped. "I almost killed ya!"

Travis' knees buckled slightly from the shock of what had happened and the surprise appearance of the stranger. Trying to regain his composure, he yelled through the wind, "Sorry, mister, but with all the snow, I was sort of lost."

His eyes squinted towards the direction of the voice, hoping to find a familiar face. It was not.

In fact, it was a scary face. Not in the horror movie sense, but a face lacking warmth. Its hollow cheeks were covered with grisly stubble, and the bloodshot eyes were cold and empty.

"Ya know," the voice continued, "I kinda saved your life by missing ya. So I guess ya owe me...big time."

Even with the high winds, Travis was able to detect the strong stench emitted by the man's clothes and body and especially his breath. It made the youngster nauseous.

"I don't know what you mean, sir," he stammered.

"Ha! I'll tell you what I mean. You're coming with me, you little..."

With that, Travis broke free of the man's grip, losing his hat in the process. He screamed, "Help!" But the fear racing through his mind scrambled the command to run fast, and instead he stumbled, falling in the deepening snow.

He was down for only a couple of seconds, but the lost momentum gave the stranger an opportunity to grab hold. Even in his inebriated state, he made the most of it. This time he wasn't letting go.

"Scream all you want, kid. There ain't no way anybody can hear you in this wind." He half carried, half dragged Travis towards his car, still idling in the storm. He opened the driver's side door and yelled at Travis to get over to the passenger's side.

Travis reluctantly crawled across the seat, appalled at the condition of the car's interior. Newspapers, empty coffee cups, donut boxes, and crumpled fast food containers were strewn about. The ashtray was open and overflowed with cigarette butts and ashes. And again, the same nauseating smell.

Travis instinctively tried to open his door and escape this nightmare.

The man cackled, "Ha-ha, you little fool. That ain't worked for years. Now quit yer' squirming. We'll be home in a few minutes."

"Home!" thought Travis. "Oh, how I wish I was home." He remained silent as the man muttered to himself while guiding the battered old car down side streets and alleys, somehow navigating through the storm until he pulled into a lane and stopped.

"Come on, kid, home sweet home. Ha-ha-ha." He grabbed Travis' arm, pulling him across the seat and out of the car.

The storm had subsided enough for Travis to see the exterior of the man's house, an old Victorian home. From what he could tell, it was in the same poor condition as the car and, for that matter, the man.

They quickly climbed the six steps, guided by the metal handrail which ran down the middle of the wide staircase. After crossing the large porch to the door, the man unlocked three dead bolts.

Travis made a last attempt to escape, but the man's hold was too strong. He was shoved into the hallway, and the door slammed closed behind them.

The driving was becoming very treacherous as Jim covered all of the surrounding neighbourhood. He checked the schoolyard and even the dugouts at the community ballpark. More than an hour had passed, and Travis was nowhere to be found. Jim phoned home from a convenience store to see if Susan had heard from their son. She hadn't.

She'd been busy phoning some of his friends to see if he had dropped in for a visit, but no one had seen or heard from Travis.

Jim decided to head home before the storm got worse. As he pulled into the driveway the wind was decreasing in strength, and he was relieved that perhaps the weather might turn in their favour. Susan was waiting at the door as he ran up the front walk.

"Heard anything yet?" he asked hopefully.

"Nothing," she replied, hugging her husband tightly. "Except when I spoke with Andy, he mentioned a fort in some ravine that they've played in since the summer. He said he'd take you there if you wanted."

Andy was the eldest son of their neighbours, the Murrays.

"Great idea. The storm seems to be letting up. Call Ian and Michelle and tell them I'm on my way to pick him up."

Jim kissed Susan and headed back down the walk. "Don't worry, I'm sure we'll find him no worse for the wear, staying at this fort." His confidence gave Susan the boost she needed, and she closed the door.

Jim was at the Murray's home in no time and honked the horn twice. Both Ian and his son, Andy, came running down the driveway.

The storm had definitely ended, and now the snow was falling in a more casual way. "Hey, I thought I'd come and help," said Ian, getting into the front seat. "I even brought a flashlight and my referee's whistle."

"Thanks. Every bit helps," replied Jim. "So, Andy, where is this secret hideaway you guys built?"

"It's in the ravine beside Archer's Park," called out Andy from the back seat, "and we only fixed it up. It was already built when we found it."

"All right then," said Jim. "We'll leave the car in the lot at the park, and you can lead us the rest of the way."

"Sure, Mr. Kirkland, and I bet that's where Travis is. You'll see," he replied confidently.

On the way Jim explained the earlier events of the evening and all the places he'd checked subsequently.

Ian recalled the time when he was a boy and had decided to run away from home, but he had had second thoughts and returned to the house. He had hidden behind the thick curtains in the dining room until he heard his mother crying with worry, then he had come out and apologized for scaring her. It had all come together with a happy ending, and he was sure tonight would turn out the same way.

But the ten-minute hike through the park to the ravine brought them to an empty lean-to. The discouraged searchers' trek back to the car seemed to take forever. While he tried to remain positive, Jim was now very, very concerned. He dropped Ian and Andy off at their house and promised to call if he needed any more help or if the situation was resolved.

The only hope now was for Travis to be back home, safe and sound, when Jim returned. But the look on Susan's face when he came through the door let him know it was not the case.

As they held on to each other, Jim was the first to

say what they both were thinking. "I guess we'd better call the police and report a missing child."

"Yes," agreed Susan, "I think you're right. Why don't you call them while I put Natalie to bed. There's no sense getting her upset by all this."

Jim put away his coat and boots as Susan went to the kitchen to get Natalie.

"Come on, honey, it's already way past your bedtime."

The two Kirkland women had finally eaten some dinner and had been washing the dishes when Jim returned.

"Is Travis with Daddy?" Natalie asked, hanging the dish towel on the inside of the cupboard door.

"No, he's...he's going to spend the night at the Murray's." Susan hated to have to tell this fib, but it fell into the white lie category.

"So when are we going to finish putting up all the decorations?" inquired Natalie, as they exited the kitchen.

"As soon as Travis is home and we can do it all together, as a family," said her mother, leading the way through the house.

They met Jim in the front hallway, and he knelt down and gave his daughter a long hug. "Good night, young lady. Sleep tight. I love you."

"I love you too, Daddy." She kissed him on the cheek and dashed up the stairs with Susan in tow.

Jim proceeded into the kitchen and sat by the phone, entering the number for the police station. He had never needed to call that number before. It rang twice.

"Station 44, police. How may I help you?" asked the policeman.

"I need to report a runaway, or I guess, a missing child," said Jim.

"Can I please have your name and address, sir?"

Jim responded with the information.

"When did you notice the child was gone?"

"Well, it was around seven o'clock, and we've been looking ever since and calling all his friends." There was an edge to his voice, a strain that the officer detected and tried to ease.

"Okay, Mr. Kirkland, now most of these cases are solved within a few hours, so don't get overly concerned. I'm going to have one of the patrol cars come around to your house shortly and get a full statement from you. Also, if you could have a photograph of your son available, that would help a lot."

"Oh sure, sure. I can get one out of the photo album. Thank you very much for your help," replied Jim.

"No problem, sir. That's why we're here. Good luck."

"Thanks. Bye." Jim hung up the receiver and immediately went to get a photo for the police.

A few years ago his call would have been noted but

held for 24 to 48 hours. However, times being what they are, the current policy is to get a description and photo out to all patrols as soon as possible.

Natalie had put on her pajamas and brushed her teeth. Her mother was reading a few pages from a storybook to her as she lay in bed. She liked to roll her tongue over the smooth enamel of her freshly polished teeth while she listened to the story.

"You know, Mommy, Travis' toothbrush is still in the bathroom, so his teeth won't feel all slippery like mine do when he goes to bed."

"No, I guess they won't," replied Susan, her mind drifting off, wondering where her older child was and if he was okay. She really didn't care if his teeth were brushed or not.

The ringing of the front doorbell caught her attention. Closing the book, she leaned towards her daughter, "Lights out, Natalie. I love you."

Natalie snuggled under the down comforter and kissed her mother, "I love you too, Mommy. Goodnight." Her eyes were closed before her mother even turned off the small lamp on the bedside table.

Susan quietly withdrew from the room, leaving the door open a few inches to let a little light from the hallway spill back into the bedroom. She came down the stairs just as Jim was opening the door.

"Good evening, Mr. Kirkland. I'm Officer Lynn Douglas. I understand your son has run away."

"That's correct," Jim nodded. "Please come in. Can we offer you a coffee?"

The policewoman stepped into the house, unbuttoning her heavy coat. "No, thank you, sir. I'd prefer to get the information and head back to the station as soon as possible. Were you able to find a photo?"

"Yes, this was taken only a couple of months ago. Is it okay?" asked Jim.

She studied the photo, then noticed Susan on the stairs, "Evening, ma'am. He's a fine-looking young fellow. You must be pretty proud of him."

"Oh, yes. We are. Very. This is so unlike him...to run away, I mean." Susan didn't want the police to think Travis was a trouble maker or that they'd had problems with him before.

"I'm sure it isn't, ma'am," the officer consoled her. "Kids at this age are experiencing new and strange emotions that can lead to some fairly unusual behaviour. All part of growing up. I'm sure we'll get this resolved. I just need to ask you a few questions, and we'll get the ball rolling."

Susan smiled and stepped closer to Jim as they answered the inquiries. Height, weight, eye colour, hair colour, clothes description...it was the standard list of characteristics needed to describe anyone. The whole process took less than ten minutes, and the officer thanked them for their cooperation and gave them her business card.

"You can call me direct at this number any time tonight, should you hear from Travis. Meanwhile, we'll get this information into the computer, and all the patrols will be on the lookout. I'll check in with you tomorrow morning before my shift ends and give you the name of my replacement, but that probably won't be necessary."

She smiled confidently, then buttoned up her coat.

Both Jim and Susan expressed their appreciation, and Jim opened the door.

"Good night, folks. I know you won't do it, but the best thing for you would be to try and get some sleep. We'll handle everything from here on."

"We'll try, Officer Douglas. Goodnight and thanks again," replied Jim. He and Susan stood together in the doorway as the policewoman walked down the path to her car.

Their attention had been so focussed on the officer and her questions that they had not noticed Natalie at the top of the stairs, listening to the exchange of information. She had quietly returned to her room and crawled under the sheets. Deeply concerned, she was thinking of Travis and his off-key, but loud, rendition of "The Twelve Days of Christmas" as she finally fell into a restless sleep.

CHAPTER THREE

New Friends, Strange Places

he moon and stars shone brightly on the blanket of clouds below. Dasher skimmed along the top of them so that it would seem just like travelling across a snow-covered field.

It was comforting to Ogilthorpe, who had to cover his eyes with his hands every time there was a break in the clouds revealing how high above the ground they actually were. As he became used to it, he started to peek out and enjoy the view. He was feeling quite pleased with himself and his plan to recover the sleigh bell. He had sung most of his favourite songs and occasionally dozed off as they raced across the sky.

After a particularly long nap, he was awakened by Dasher's snorting. Rubbing the sleep from his eyes and stretching a big yawn, he inquired about their arrival time.

"Are we finally there, Dasher?"

"Ah-h ro-o-o!" replied the reindeer, nodding his head and beginning their descent through the clouds. The snow was falling lightly on the sleepy city below.

The wind currents surrounding the sleigh attracted the snow like a magnet, creating a miniature snowstorm that camouflaged their flight path to the rooftop of the Kirkland home. Dasher's surefootedness provided a smooth landing, and Ogilthorpe, still hidden by the swirling snow, climbed out of the sleigh and patted Dasher's nose.

"Great job, old friend. Hold tight. I'll be back in a jiffy."

With that, he concentrated, and once again the tips of his ears began to vibrate to the frequency of the bell. This time, Ogilthorpe magically disappeared and then reappeared in Travis' bedroom. Much to the surprise of the tiny elf, there was no sound of a sleeping child, and his still vibrating ears should have caused the missing bell to ring in response.

Instead, it was quiet. "My goodness," thought Ogilthorpe, "how could that be? I know this is the right place, and the bell and Travis should be here."

"He runned away," sniffled a voice.

The sound of a human caused his ears to stop vibrating, and the tassel on the end of his floppy knitted cap stood straight up in the air. He turned around and looked up at the face of Natalie.

"How did you know what I was thinking?" he whispered.

She stepped closer and bent down. "I dunno. I just heard it...after I heard the ringing noise," she replied.

He remembered Santa saying how sometimes he encounters children during his visits, and it is because they believe so deeply in the magic of Christmas. Some children hear the sleigh bells or the sounds of the reindeer on the roof, and others are sure they see Santa fill their stockings or disappear up the chimney.

But Ogilthorpe had never heard of anybody able to read thoughts.

"You're Travis' sister, Natalie, aren't you?" he asked.

"That's right. But you don't look like I thought you'd look, Santa," she lamented.

"He-he-he!" he giggled. "I'm not Santa. My name is Ogilthorpe, currently Stablemaster responsible for reindeer, sleighs and harnesses." He was very proud of this designation.

"Then it *was* one of Santa's sleigh bells. Oh, I knew it! I knew it the second I saw it. An' Travis laughed at me and didn't believe it."

"Yes, Natalie, you are right. It is a magic sleigh bell. But it should be here in this house, and it's not. You say Travis ran away. Do you think he took it with him?"

"I don't know. He might have." She then proceeded to explain everything that had happened since they'd discovered the bell. Ogilthorpe listened intently. He felt a strong connection with Natalie and decided that, indeed, she was special. Her belief in the magic of Christmas was so deep that it was almost like being with another elf. He wanted to help her as much as she wanted to help him.

"If you just find Travis, he'll give you back the bell, I'm sure."

"It's not that simple, Natalie. I need to use one of Santa's Magic Snowballs, and they are back at the North Pole. My, my, this is getting most complicated. I'll have to return up north and get Santa to find out where Travis is. I probably should have asked for his help in the first place, but I didn't want to be a bother, especially with Christmas so close. We're so very busy these days."

"Oh, it must be wonderful! Are there lots of elves? How many? How many?" she inquired excitedly.

"Well now, I've never given that much thought. Let's see..."

He paused, counting in his head, then gave a typical elf answer.

"There's certainly more than a few, but less than too many. It's rather multitudinous, actually, which is as numerous as we need."

Natalie was puzzled by this response, but after giving it consideration, she was totally satisfied with it. "That's about how many I thought," she said, slowly nodding her head.

A true believer.

She had many other questions to ask but knew they

would have to wait. It was important that her new friend begin his journey back.

"Will you come back here? And will Santa come this time?" she asked.

"I really can't say. Anything is possible. One thing is certain, Santa will know what to do," he assured her.

"Well then, you'd better get going. It was very nice to meet you, Ogilthorpe. Good-bye and have a Merry Christmas."

Removing his hat and bowing deeply, he responded, "It was all my pleasure, Natalie. Thank you for your help, and a very Merry Christmas to you."

His ears started vibrating as soon as he placed his hat on his head. Right before her very eyes, he vanished into thin air. She ran to the window, hoping to see him crossing the sky, but the only thing she saw was a swirling mass of snow.

While Natalie's concerns had been calmed by Ogilthorpe's appearance during the night, Travis' experience had not been as reassuring.

Once inside the building, with the locks on the door engaged again, the strange man continued to mumble and complain about everything.

He'd inherited the large, old mansion many years ago and had divided it into rental apartments to help pay the bills.

"Ain't nobody here no more, so it's just gonna be you and me," he growled. "Come on, my place is on the second floor."

He pushed Travis towards the steep bank of stairs which led to the darkened upper level.

"You better let me go, mister. My parents are going to be worried about me," protested Travis.

"Ha-ha-ha!" the man cackled, grabbing the collar on Travis' coat and directing him up the stairs. "Your parents couldn't care less about you. Otherwise, you wouldn't be wandering around in a blizzard, at night, in a lousy neighbourhood. You probably cause all sorts of problems, and they're happy to be rid of you. What you need is a little discipline, and that's exactly what I'll give you if you don't listen to me. So be quiet and behave yourself."

The man opened his apartment door, turning the light switch on as they entered. Travis hardly had an opportunity to look around before he was pushed into another small, dark room.

"Make yourself at home, kid. I'll be back in a while."

The man hit the light switch before closing the door. Travis heard the clicking of a lock as he stood staring at his new home. The room was like everything else associated with the stranger...a filthy mess.

A single, lumpy mattress lay on the floor, no springs or frame to support it. Against one wall leaned an old chrome chair with a padded plastic seat and backrest. The only window was nailed shut, and the layers of dirt and grime on the glass gave it a frosted coating, so it was impossible to see in or out. Travis walked over to another door in hopes of finding an escape route, but it was only a closet, empty, except for a couple of wire hangers.

Tossing his knapsack inside, he went back to sit on the mattress, too scared to cry, too tired to think straight. Things had gone from bad to worse. The spilled hot chocolate seemed pretty minor compared to the mess he was in now.

If only he and Natalie had never taken out the Christmas decorations, he thought, none of this would have happened. "Christmas...just a stupid holiday for little kids. My parents don't want to celebrate Christmas, and they probably are happy to be rid of me, just like the man said."

A sad, confused Travis lay back on the mattress and fell asleep.

In the kitchen of the dingy apartment, Cuthbert MacIntyre sat at the table and pondered his actions. The ever-present cigarette burned slowly as it dangled from his dry, cracked lips. The smudged glass of whiskey still sat on the table where he'd left it earlier in the evening, before he'd ventured out into the storm for more cigarettes. He reached over with a slightly trembling hand and drank the beverage in one huge gulp. His alcohol-induced haze gave meaning and sense to his rambling thoughts. "A kid around the place is what I've always needed. Someone to go out in bad weather and run errands for me. Grocery shopping, laundry, yard work...yeah, all sorts of things. Just because I've never found the right woman to marry and start a family with, doesn't mean I shouldn't have a kid."

It all made sense to him in a sad way. This selfish, mean-spirited man was totally alone in the world, without a friend or relative. But it was all his own doing.

The last tenant had moved out more than a year before, tired of the unanswered requests for a cleaner building with dependable plumbing.

The last few months had been a tragic descent into a worsening existence. Cuthbert's days consisted mostly of sleeping on the couch and mindlessly staring at soap operas, talk shows, and tabloid news programs. His few trips into the neighbourhood were only to replenish the vices he so readily indulged in.

The overall effect of this chosen lifestyle was that he looked and moved like an elderly man, though he was not yet 60. His behaviour was such that he would have disgusted even himself a few years ago. But now, everything was justifiable, and he even considered himself a hero for rescuing the boy from the snowstorm. "Why, I'll even train the lad to respect older people and property. Not like those other neighbourhood kids who taunt me and throw stones at my windows. Maybe he's one of those brats...well, I'll make an example of him. But first I'd better feed him something."

Even though it was now quite late, he quickly made a peanut butter and jam sandwich and grabbed a soda out of the fridge. Approaching Travis' room, he took the old-fashioned key out of his shirt pocket and unlocked the door.

"Hey, kid," he yelled, "here's something to eat."

Travis sat up and reached out, managing to mumble a thank you as he took the food.

"What's your name, kid?"

"Travis, Travis Kirkland," he replied.

"Well, Travis, my name is Cuthbert MacIntyre, and since I saved your life tonight, it's now mine to do whatever I want with," he declared, swaying slightly in the doorway. "An' what I want is for you to be the son I never had. So from now on, your name is MacIntyre, Travis MacIntyre. Got it?"

"Yes, Mr. MacIntyre," Travis reluctantly agreed.

"You dumb kid," hissed Cuthbert, leaning forward. "You don't call me MISTER MacIntyre. You just say SIR!"

"Ye-yes, sir." Travis was wide awake now, and he trembled with fear.

"That's better. Now eat your food and get some sleep 'cause tomorrow you'll learn all the chores you get to do."

With that, Cuthbert stepped backward, slamming the door shut. After locking the door, he placed the key back in his shirt pocket. Staggering to the kitchen, he made himself a sandwich and poured another drink.

Travis was reeling from this latest encounter, but his rumbling stomach quickly turned his attention to the sandwich. He wasted no time in devouring it, and then washed the crumbs down with the soda. He was too tired and depressed to plan his escape, and for the first time since this whole episode began, he felt tears filling his eyes. They ran down his cheeks and dropped onto the mattress as he lay back, encouraging sleep, in the hope that all of this would turn out to be just a bad dream.

Natalie woke up the next morning with a renewed optimism and immediately began humming and singing Christmas songs. She had slept wonderfully, dreaming about elves and reindeer.

After washing her face and combing her hair, she quickly dressed and came down the stairs. She smiled at all the boxes and decorations still waiting to be attended to, as she skipped to the kitchen.

"Good morning, Mommy. Good morning, Daddy!" she cheerfully said, bursting through the doorway.

"Sh-h-h, good morning, honey. Daddy's on the phone. Come and sit down," instructed her mother.

"That's right...sure. No, I understand...I'd appreciate that very much, Officer Douglas. Thank you. Bye," said Jim, hanging up the phone and shaking his head in disappointment.

"Guess what happened last night, Daddy?" bubbled Natalie.

"That's nice," said Jim, not really listening to what she'd said.

"Look, Natalie, we've got a serious situation here, and your mother and I want to tell you about it."

Both Jim and Susan looked awful. They hadn't left the kitchen all night. The first couple of hours were spent waiting for the phone or doorbell to ring with good news. It never happened.

They then devised a plan to organize a search for Travis. They made lists of friends to contact with telephone numbers and addresses. The phone and fax numbers for all the local radio stations, television stations and newspapers had been obtained. A step-by-step process had been developed to ensure that everything that could possibly be done, would be.

They had dozed off in their chairs occasionally but awoke with a renewed energy and commitment each time. Everything would depend on the feedback from the police in the morning.

The phone call had provided that, and now it was necessary to put their plan into operation.

"I know, Daddy," Natalie declared matter-of-factly. "Travis runned away."

Susan and Jim were shocked by their daughter's statement. They assumed she knew nothing about it.

"How do you know that? Did Travis talk to you? Is there something you're not telling us?" said Jim.

"No, Travis didn't tell me. I heard you talking to the policewoman at the front door. But everything is going to be all right."

They misunderstood her statement of fact as just a reassuring thought and tried to reinforce that feeling. "Yes, honey, everything will turn out fine. The police are helping, and Travis will be found," said Susan.

"But we don't need the police. Ogilthorpe is going to find him."

"Ogilthorpe? Is that a friend of Travis' we don't know?" asked Jim, scanning the list of names. "What's his phone number?"

Natalie couldn't hold her laughter. "Daddy, Ogilthorpe doesn't have a phone. He's an elf!"

"He's a what?" questioned Jim.

"You know, an elf...at the North Pole...they help Santa. Ogilthorpe is the Stablemaster in charge of rein-deers and...stuff. He was in Travis' room last night looking for the bell we found in the leaves."

"Oh, great," sighed Jim, believing Natalie's imagination was hard at work. "Well, in the meantime, your mother and I have developed a plan to let people know Travis may be lost and that we want everyone's help in finding him. Even...Ogilthorpe's." He gently patted her hand. "We're just putting the finishing touches on an information poster that we're going to distribute so people will be able to recognize your brother and let us know if they've seen him. I'm going to type it up now and take it to the copy centre to have lots of copies made."

Jim headed down to his basement office, and Susan made breakfast for Natalie. This was the first day of the Christmas school break, so there was no rush to get Natalie organized and ready.

Considering the circumstances, she wouldn't have been going anyway.

Natalie chattered about Christmas, the decorations and elves. Susan let her ramble on because she felt it was better than having her worry about Travis.

Jim was coming back up the stairs when the front doorbell rang. Their hearts all skipped a beat at the sound, in anticipation of the news it would bring. There was a sense of restrained urgency as they hurried to answer the door. Susan opened it to find Officer Douglas on the front porch. Alone.

"Good morning, Mrs. Kirkland. May I come in?"

Susan was trying desperately to interpret the concerned look on her face. "Certainly, Officer Douglas."

"I thought your shift was finished?" said Jim.

"It is, sir, but I wanted to bring this personally for your verification." She reached into her pocket and pulled out the red and white striped knit hat. "It matched the description and..."

"That's Travis' hat," said Susan, grabbing it and studying it closely, wishing it could talk and tell her what had happened to her son.

"Where did you find it?" asked Jim.

"One of the patrol cars noticed it in a snow bank, on Burrows Avenue, just after sunrise."

"Burrows Avenue?" both Jim and Susan said.

"What would he be doing way down there?" asked Susan.

"We can't be sure, but it's past the turn-off for Archer's Park and the fort you mentioned. He possibly went too far in the storm and became disoriented. After that...well, it's hard to say at this point." Her voice drifted off in disappointment. She had hoped it wouldn't be Travis' hat.

"Susan and I have developed a plan to let as many people as possible know what's happened, and we'd like to put it into action," stated Jim.

Officer Douglas nodded in agreement.

"The Department appreciates any effort to help us

get the community involved. If you'd like, I'll stay a while to review your plan and coordinate it with our established procedures on dealing with a missing or abducted child."

It was the first time anyone had used the term abducted, and it raised the seriousness of the situation to a higher level.

"Let me take your coat, Officer," offered Jim. "You're going to be here for a while."

Travis stared at the ceiling. He had been awake since the morning light filtered through the dirty window. A strange calm had come over him as he evaluated his situation. He would prepare for the opportunity to escape, should one present itself, but in the meantime, he would try his best not to provoke Cuthbert MacIntyre.

He shivered at the thought of his captor. "Perhaps," he wondered, "the old guy might have second thoughts about his actions and will let me go today. But then, I'll still be in trouble with my parents for running away and causing so many problems."

The click of the key turning the lock brought his attention back to the door, which swung open to reveal a stern-looking Cuthbert MacIntyre looming above him.

"Enough lying around, kid. Here's your breakfast," he said, tossing a peanut butter sandwich onto the mattress. "The bathroom is across the hall if you need to use it. You got five minutes, and then it's up to the third floor. You're starting with a bucket of soapy water, and you can scrub the hallway walls and floor. We need to spruce the joint up if we want to get some more suckers...uh, I mean tenants, to pay rent. Ha-ha!" Cuthbert relished the thought of once again cashing the cheques. "End of the month and not a second late or they're out on the sidewalk. You gotta be tough with 'em, kid, or they'll walk all over you. That's lesson number one. Now, hurry up!"

Travis stuffed the sandwich into his mouth and chewed as rapidly as the thick peanut butter would allow. As soon as he finished he went in to use the bathroom and, after washing up, timidly made his way into the living room.

Stacks of newspapers and magazines were everywhere. Unopened mail and full ashtrays spilled onto the floor. The television was on, but the picture was erratic...clear, then snowy, then squiggly, then clear again. It made the only sound in the apartment. Travis couldn't believe that anyone would actually live in such a mess. He gazed across the room into the adjacent kitchen, and there sat Cuthbert.

The man's nicotine-stained fingers were rubbing his

temples in a desperate attempt to ease the constant throbbing from his ever-present headache. It took him a few seconds before he realized his young captive was watching.

"Hey," he growled, "whadda you lookin' at?"

"Nothing, sir," replied Travis. "I'm ready to start my chores."

"No, you're not. The bucket and brush are under the sink. Get 'em!" Cuthbert ordered.

Travis quickly entered the kitchen and opened the cupboard door, revealing an old metal pail and a large scrub brush.

"Now, fill it with hot water and some detergent!"

Travis obeyed the commands, and together they left the apartment and climbed the upper stairs.

"Start at that end and work towards me," pointed Cuthbert. "I'll be watching you." With that, he slid down the wall onto the floor at the top of the staircase, effectively blocking any exit.

Travis walked down the dimly lit hall and started to scrub the walls. It immediately reminded him of yesterday with his family, mopping up the hot chocolate. He took a deep breath and scrubbed harder, determined not to let his emotions overwhelm him. After a few minutes he stopped and looked up towards the ceiling. "Excuse me, sir, but I'll need a ladder or stool to reach the top of the walls," he said.

Cuthbert thought for a moment and considered just

using a weaker light bulb to help hide the dirt, but he figured that as long as the kid was around, he might as well use him. "Okay, I'll get a chair from the apartment...keep working!"

There was a folding step ladder in the basement workshop, but he didn't feel like climbing all those stairs nor did he trust Travis to go down there. So he got a chair from his living room and returned to the third floor. Tossing it down the hall, he yelled, "No more interruptions or talking until you've finished."

He resumed his position barricading the top of the staircase. Though his breathing was quite laboured as a result of the stair climbing, he lit up a cigarette and pondered the other chores he'd have Travis do. The scratching of the scrub brush and dripping of water into the pail were the last sounds he heard before settling into his regular morning snooze.

The ride back to the North Pole was not the triumphant journey Ogilthorpe had envisioned when he'd first set out. Instead of the magic sleigh bell, he had only an empty, sad feeling in his heart. This was a new emotion for him, as elves are usually very cheerful, and he didn't like being this way one bit.

It wasn't just that he didn't get the sleigh bell. It

was that Travis had run away, and his family was now so concerned and unhappy. To be that way was terrible, especially at Christmas time. "How awful," thought Ogilthorpe. "Come on, Dasher, we've no time to lose," he yelled out. "We must hurry and see Santa."

"Ah-h ro-o-o!" called the reindeer. Just the mention of Santa's name gave him extra energy to skip along the clouds.

The sun was already up and shining when they began their descent into Santa's Village. Many of the elves were gathered in the courtyard in front of the stable as the tiny sleigh touched down and came to a halt. Ogilthorpe was quite surprised as they rushed forward to greet him.

Dudley was the first to reach the sleigh. "Oh, Ogilthorpe, are you okay? We were so worried when you didn't come to the bunkhouse last night."

"Yes, that's right," agreed Knickerbocker. "We thought perhaps you'd had an accident." All the elves nodded in agreement. Ogilthorpe was really quite embarrassed that he had caused his friends to worry.

"I'm very sorry. This most definitely was not my intention. Oh dear, oh dear!" he lamented.

At that moment, Santa himself stepped out of his workshop and came across the courtyard. The elves cleared a path for him to approach the sleigh.

"My, my, Ogilthorpe, what's this I hear about you staying out all night long?" he teased.

"All night!" exclaimed Ogilthorpe. "I only went to get a missing sleigh bell that had finally been rung three times. I was sure I would be back before bedtime. After all, Santa, you visit all the good children in one night!"

"Ho-ho-ho!" laughed Santa, which brought big smiles to the faces of the elves. "Of course I do, because eight reindeer can fly much faster together than only one alone. It's a benefit of teamwork," he declared.

The gathered elves nodded in agreement. Teamwork is one of the secrets for success in Santa's Village.

"Come now, everyone, Ogilthorpe's adventure is over and there's plenty of work to get done today. So off we go, and remember to...have a great day!" All the elves joined in together and loudly heralded one of Santa's favourite sayings. It was one of the morale boosters that he was so good at. Everyone returned to their duties with renewed vitality.

As Ogilthorpe climbed out of the sleigh, he called to Santa. "As soon as I put Dasher in his stall and feed him, I'd like to come and talk to you. It's quite important."

"Then, come with me now," said Santa. "Mortimer, would you please unhitch Dasher and put away the sleigh. Oh, and give him some extra feed. He's had his exercise for the day."

"Certainly, Santa," said the young stable apprentice, "I'm most happy to help."

Santa and Ogilthorpe walked back to the workshop. "So, you must be tired after your long trip," said Santa.

"Not really," replied Ogilthorpe. "I was able to nap along the way. Dasher made sure it was a smooth flight."

"That's good. Now, what's so important?" inquired Santa as they entered the workshop. Ogilthorpe slowly took off his coat and hung it on the rack of antlers. He was thinking of how best to tell Santa about the runaway boy.

"Well, Santa," he said hesitantly, "my trip was unsuccessful. When I arrived at the house of the young boy who had found the bell, it was too late."

"What do you mean, too late?" asked Santa, settling into his well-worn leather reading chair.

"It seems he ran away from home and took the bell with him. I met his sister, and she told me all about him. She is a very special girl, for she could hear me vibrating my ears and even read my thoughts!"

"Hm-m-m!" pondered Santa. "What are their names? And then, please tell me the whole story."

"They are Travis and Natalie Kirkland."

"Ho-ho-ho, of course, I remember Natalie very well. She really loves Christmas!" said Santa. "But now that you mention them, I don't recall getting a letter from either one this year."

"That's right. I checked the book last night and nothing's been received so far, but Natalie assured me they were just mailed."

Santa listened intently as Ogilthorpe repeated the whole story of the missing bell and how it had been found at the Kirkland house. He spoke softly when he mentioned the difficulties the family was having and Travis' subsequent disappearance.

Santa occasionally shook his head and sighed as he heard the details. He was always saddened when he learned of people's troubles, and it served to strengthen his resolve to bring a little bit of happiness into their lives.

"...so, like I told Natalie, you would know what to do. Then I got in the sleigh, and Dasher took off as fast as he could."

Ogilthorpe paused and waited for Santa to respond. The crackling of the burning logs in the massive stone fireplace joined the rhythmic ticking of the mantle clock. Santa scratched his head and stroked his soft white beard, as he often did when he was deep in thought. Ogilthorpe had been witness to this ritual many times.

Finally, he spoke. "If it was just the bell, I'd be inclined to delay its retrieval until after the busy season, but..." he paused, recalling some of his previous visits to the Kirkland house and how he had always felt a special Christmas spirit when he was there. "For Travis to be missing must be terrible for the whole family. What would you suggest be done, Ogilthorpe?" Santa often involved the elves in various decisions, and he valued their input regarding all matters in the village.

"Well, between snoozes on the trip, I did give it a little thought, and it might be advantageous for us to check on Travis' whereabouts by consulting a Magic Snowball. Then I thought we could go get him and the bell, and everyone would be happy."

"Easier said than done," counselled Santa, "but I agree in general, so let's see where Travis is hiding out."

Ogilthorpe beamed as they got up from their chairs and went over to the high ledger desk. Santa reached over and opened the window. Resting on the ledge was an assortment of snowballs. He took the first one in his hand and packed it tight, smoothing the edges over and over until it started to glow. He placed it on the ledge, and suddenly it became crystal clear.

Santa concentrated on Travis and waited for an image to appear, but nothing happened. He thought a moment, frowned, then reached for another larger snowball and repeated the procedure, concentrating even harder. Much to his dismay, nothing happened again.

Santa turned to Ogilthorpe and sadly explained,

"I'm very sorry, my friend, but I'm unable to get an image of Travis. It seems he no longer believes in me or the magic of Christmas."

Ogilthorpe was shocked whenever this happened. "How can people stop believing?" he would always say. "Christmas is so wonderful that its spirit can carry a person right through the whole year. But they have to keep believing."

The saddest thing was that it meant they would not be able to reunite the Kirkland family. "Oh, Santa," said Ogilthorpe, "I promised to help Natalie. She was really looking forward to a great Christmas."

"Now, now. Don't become too disheartened. This whole matter might resolve itself. After all, there was no guarantee that we could have helped Travis, even if we had found him. Remember, we are very limited in what we are able to do when we travel outside of the North Pole."

"I know, Santa." Ogilthorpe let out a big sigh of disappointment and slowly shook his head. He so wanted to help Natalie by finding Travis.

"Here's what I'll do," said Santa. "Every once in a while, I'll check in on Natalie and see what the situation is. And I'll keep you informed. It's the best we can do for now, Ogilthorpe. So let's keep a positive outlook. Meanwhile, there's lots of work left to do in preparation for this year's big trip. You know I'm counting on you to have the reindeer in shape and the harness and sleigh all polished and ready to go." He put his hand on Ogilthorpe's shoulder and gave him a reassuring squeeze.

Ogilthorpe felt a little better and smiled up at Santa. "I most definitely will have everything ready. In fact, I'm going to go and do an extra soap oil treatment on the harness right now!" He ran to the door and grabbed his coat. "There will never be another lost bell as long as I'm Stablemaster," he declared, grabbing a candy cane as he departed Santa's Workshop.

Santa was pleased that his little friend was getting back in the spirit, and he let out a tiny ho-ho-ho that built itself into a full-blown, tummy-jiggling laugh that reverberated through the whole village and reminded everyone that Christmas Eve was coming soon.

Officer Douglas was very impressed with Susan and Jim's plan. She made a couple of suggestions and then called the police station to get final approval before leaving. Her extra efforts were greatly appreciated by the Kirklands.

It was now mid-morning, and Jim was preparing to leave the house.

"I'll get a hundred copies made on the way to the arena," he explained to Susan as he put on his coat.

There was a special Christmas holiday practice session for Travis' hockey team that Jim helped coach. Susan had come up with the idea of advising everyone at the arena about their son's disappearance and then enlisting any volunteers. It was a quick way to get a lot of people who knew the Kirkland family involved in helping them out.

"Don't forget to pick up Ian and Andy on the way," reminded Susan.

Ian had called and said he was taking some time off work to help in whatever way they needed. He was certainly a good friend.

"Don't worry, that's on my to-do list." Jim always made lists. "We are going to find Travis, and everything is going to be all right." He hugged his wife and held her tightly, each drawing strength from the other. "I love you," he said.

"I love you, too," she replied. "Now get going. I've got a lot of calls to make." Susan's assignment was to contact all the newspapers, radio and television stations, bring them up to date on the situation and recruit their involvement.

"I'll call in every hour or so. Bye-bye," said Jim as he headed out the door.

He picked up the Murrays, had the photocopies made and was at the arena in half an hour. He spoke with the arena manager and was given permission to talk to the players and parents over the public address system. He stepped onto the ice and, with the microphone in hand, made his plea.

"Attention, everyone. Could I have your attention, please?" There were a few hoots and hollers, as they were in a holiday mood and thought Jim was just fooling around or making some boring announcement.

"Hey, Mr. Kirkland, sing us a Christmas song!" yelled out Ethan O'Connor.

"Okay, Jim, that's a two-minute penalty for unsportsmanlike conduct. Ha-ha-ha!" joked Keith Burke, a fellow hockey dad.

Even Jim couldn't help smiling at the friendly kidding. But he had serious business to talk about, and he raised his hand to quiet the crowd.

"I'm sorry to interrupt the practice, but there is something very important I need to talk to all of you about. My name is Jim Kirkland, for those of you who don't know me. My son is Travis Kirkland, number 4 for the Greenfield Hornets."

The kids all cheered at the mention of their team. Jim waited for the noise to subside.

"Travis has been missing since seven o'clock last evening."

The whole arena became quiet. Everyone's full attention was focussed on the solitary figure standing on the ice.

"We are not sure what happened, but if anybody has any information that could help us find him, it would be greatly appreciated."

There was slight murmuring as everyone looked around, hoping someone else would step forward. But nothing happened, and the eerie silence returned.

"The police have been notified and are doing all that they can. However, my wife and I have devised a plan to search for Travis and inform the whole community about his disappearance. We will be looking for volunteers to help us with neighbourhood-by-neighbourhood searches and flyer distribution. We realize that most of you are busy preparing for Christmas, but any help you could give would be appreciated. I'll be available in the arena snack bar during and after practice to take down the names and phone numbers of anybody interested in helping. Thank you for your time and have a Merry Christmas."

His voice got very strained and almost cracked with emotion on the last sentence. He turned and walked off the ice and headed under the stands. Ian was waiting for him and, by the time they left the dressing room area and climbed up the stairs to the snack room, people were already forming a line to sign up.

There were parents, brothers, sisters, teenagers, kids still in their hockey equipment. Why, even the arena manager and the Zamboni driver were in the line.

It was the greatest sight Jim had ever seen.

He and Ian immediately began setting up a desk and the street map that Susan had sectioned off earlier. It was their intention to appoint a coordinator in each section who lived in that neighbourhood and would organize the volunteers. What they needed now were people's names, phone numbers and which section they lived in. Those who qualified and agreed to be coordinators would be called back in the afternoon to arrange to pick up a list of volunteers, as well as a supply of information flyers.

"Jim, I'm really sorry about the joking around when you started to speak," an embarrassed Keith Burke said from his spot at the head of the line. "What can I do to help with this crowd?"

"No apology necessary, Keith," assured Jim. "I needed the laugh. Pull up another desk and chair. Get each person's name and phone number, as well as what section they live in according to this map."

He pointed to the map Ian was taping to the wall behind them so everyone could see. In no time at all the three friends were filling pages with the necessary information.

Jim looked up and saw another familiar face.

"Mr. Kirkland, I'm very sorry to learn of your problem," said Bettyann Greenfield, owner of the company that sponsored Travis' hockey team. "I just popped over to watch the practice and wish a Merry Christmas to everyone. But your distressing announcement certainly caught my attention. You seem to have things well under control."

"We're trying our best, Ms. Greenfield," replied Jim.

"Well, if there's anything I can do, I want you to call me. Correction, here's what I can offer now, and if you need more, tell me. First, here's my cellular phone. Use it as much as you need." She handed it to Jim and continued in her no-nonsense way. "Second, you mentioned flyers...how many copies do you have?"

"One hundred," said Jim, still holding the phone.

"Then give me one, and I'll get a few hundred more within an hour. If you agree, I'll get a temporary phone number so all calls can come to a central location. Have you thought about where you want to locate?" she asked.

"We assumed we'd do it out of the house," replied Jim.

"I can free up some office space, if you'd prefer?" she offered.

"Why not right here?" said Bill Burelle. He was the arena manager and had been listening from his place in line. "It's centrally located to the community, everyone knows where it is, and there's lots of parking. Heck, if no one's going to be using the place because they're helping you, we might as well pitch in too."

"Sounds great to me," said an overwhelmed Jim.

"This will be perfect," said Ian. "Why don't you go over your plan with Ms. Greenfield and get her input. I can get some others to help Keith and me with the name collecting."

"Okay, but first I want to touch base with Susan." He was about to get up and go to the pay phone, when he remembered the cellular phone in his hand. He punched in his home number and waited for her to answer. "Honey," he said, "you aren't going to believe the response we got."

It was quite obvious to Travis that the washing of the walls and floors was not going to greatly improve the appearance or condition of the building. The cracks in the plaster and the gouges and scratches in the woodwork were still going to be there. But if this is what his captor wanted, then this is what he'd do.

The morning passed rather quickly, and he was almost finished the upper level. He had slowly worked his way towards a snoozing Cuthbert.

The water in the bucket was now so filthy that he was just rearranging the dirt on the walls. Travis coughed loudly a couple of times to awaken the wheezing figure at the top of the stairs. It wasn't enough, and the snoring continued. Finally Travis called out, "Excuse me, sir!"

That worked, and slowly Cuthbert began to collect his wits about him and opened his eyes. His first glance was directly down the steep staircase, and this gave him quite a scare as he temporarily forgot where he was. He almost lost his balance and instinctively grabbed the handrail to brace himself, while waiting for his thoughts to get organized. "What? What is it?" he yelled out.

"Behind you, sir. I need clean water," said Travis.

"Oh yeah...you! I'm not lugging that bucket around for ya'. Follow me, and we'll go back to the apartment." He pulled himself up and started down the stairs, which triggered a coughing fit that continued right into the kitchen. He lit a cigarette which only irritated his lungs further, and he continued hacking and snorting as Travis dumped out and refilled the bucket.

"How far did ya' get, kid?"

"I'm almost at the top of the stairs. It's taking longer than I thought it would," replied Travis.

"Well, you ain't paid to think now, are ya'. In fact, you ain't being paid at all! Ha-ha!" His laughter set off more coughing spasms, so he pushed Travis back to the stairs.

In between gasps for air, he instructed Travis to climb back up to the third floor, finish that level, then work his way back down the staircase to where Cuthbert was lazily settling his body to resume his interrupted snooze.

There was no time for snoozing or cat naps at the North Pole. Santa's Village was now operating at top speed. All the elves were busy doing their jobs, secure in the knowledge that they were contributing towards another successful Christmas season.

Already, they were beginning to fill Santa's magic sack with gifts for all the good girls and boys. And although it looked like even one more candy cane would cause it to rupture and spill all the presents onto the snowy courtyard, there was always room for more.

Ogilthorpe and the stable's apprentice elves had finished the morning exercise session with the reindeer. Takeoffs and landings had been picture perfect as the team grew more excited in anticipation of the upcoming trip. Mortimer and the other apprentices were brushing the gleaming coats of the reindeer before putting them back into their stalls. "We can finish up here, Ogilthorpe. I know you want to get over to Santa's Workshop for an update on Natalie and Travis."

"Why, thank you, Mortimer. It has been in the back of my mind all morning. Please remember to polish Donder's right antler. It was looking a little dull to me. I'll be back in a while, and we'll begin a harness inspection."

He ran across the courtyard and paused only once to fall back into an untouched patch of snow, creating an angel silhouette. He then jumped up, shook the snow off his backside and proceeded over to see Santa.

As he entered the workshop, the elves were busy sorting and opening mail that was received around the clock. They were bustling to make sure all the letters were read and that any special requests were noted for Santa to take into consideration.

Occasionally, it was necessary for Santa to use a Magic Snowball to verify that somebody really did need that new hockey stick or ballet shoes that they requested. Or if someone mentioned in their letter that they had been sick recently, he always liked to check that they were feeling better.

"I thought we'd be seeing you about now," said Santa, without even lifting his eyes from the letter he was reading.

"It was most difficult not to leave the reindeer's morning exercise, Santa," exclaimed Ogilthorpe, as he removed his coat. "I've been thinking of Natalie and poor Travis ever since I returned."

"Well then, we'd better not wait another second." With that, he took a snowball from the window ledge. In an instant, he was looking at Natalie and her mother as they arrived inside the arena to the command post that had been set up. "My, my, they certainly have organized the community to help search for Travis. It looks like a lot of people are getting involved. Hm-m, why there's Paul Belton. He didn't make it to the list of good boys this year, but I think we can add him back on now. Most definitely." Santa smiled as he always did when he was able to keep someone on the list.

"Pardon me, Santa, but these just came in with the latest delivery. I know you wanted to get them right away." It was Orval, the administrative assistant in the workshop. He handed two envelopes to Santa. "Good afternoon, Ogilthorpe. We're all keeping our fingers crossed that Natalie's brother will be found soon."

"That is most gracious of you, Orval. Thank you."

"Yes, Orval, and thank you for getting these." Santa turned and indicated to Ogilthorpe. "They're from Natalie and Travis. Let's see if they can give us any clues." Santa carefully read each. Then, passing them to Ogilthorpe, he shook his head and began to stroke his beard. "Nothing out of the ordinary. It's surprising that Travis could write such a nice letter, even making a point of reminding me that his sister has been very good this year. And now he's lost the Christmas spirit, and we can't even find him with a Magic Snowball. Tsk, tsk, tsk."

Ogilthorpe didn't like to see Santa so disappointed. "Well, as you say, this whole terrible situation has managed to bring people together and, with all that love and good effort, I'm starting to feel pretty confident that they will be able to get this mystery solved."

"Now, there's the right attitude," said Santa with a twinkle in his eye. "I've got to get back to these letters, and I think you're heading up a harness inspection..."

"Say-y-y, how did you know that?" smiled Ogilthorpe, knowing perfectly well that Santa knows everything that goes on in the village.

"Ho-ho-ho!" chuckled Santa as he returned to his letters. And he was still smiling as Ogilthorpe paused on his way out the door and grabbed a handful of peppermint candy canes to take back for the elves in the stable.

CHAPTER FOUR

True Believers

he harsh glare from the television lights caused Natalie to squint her eyes. She and her parents were sitting patiently at the far end of the room waiting to video an appeal that would appear on one of the local television stations.

Susan had arranged it earlier, agreeing to meet with the camera crew at the headquarters set up in the arena. She had already done three radio interviews, and a reporter from the morning paper was waiting to talk with her and Jim.

It was all part of the master plan they had devised to use every means possible to let everyone know about Travis. They hoped that somewhere, someone had seen or heard something that would lead to his return.

"Mommy, how come we don't have to put on any make-up if we're going to be on T.V.?" asked Natalie.

"That's only for T.V. stars, honey. This is just to help find Travis," explained Susan.

At the other end of the room, twenty volunteers were updating the schedule of neighbourhoods that had been canvassed that afternoon. Already they were receiving phone calls from concerned people offering to be of assistance in the search. A couple of callers thought they had seen a child fitting Travis' description, and their names were passed on to the police to be interviewed.

A caterer had just dropped off some sandwich trays, soft drinks and coffee, courtesy of Bettyann Greenfield. Earlier she had made good on the offer of additional phone lines to help handle the increasing flow of information.

She never hesitated to help people in the community. Her success in life was because she worked very hard and surrounded herself with the best people, who truly enjoyed what they did.

She always managed, however, to donate time, resources and finances to everything from minor hockey teams to major hospital fund raising. As sponsor for Travis' team, she would occasionally come to watch games and lend some vocal support. A recent widow, whose two children were away at university, she enjoyed cheering on the kids and sharing an occasional cup of hot chocolate with some of the parents.

She had chatted informally with Susan and Jim over the course of the hockey season and had always enjoyed seeing them. She admired their strength during this difficult time and was glad to be able to help.

It had also given her an opportunity to get to know

Jim better, and she was surprised to learn of his difficulty in finding employment. Thinking about the new
division she was planning to open, she believed Jim
might be an excellent choice to hire as the general
manager. His marketing and administrative experience were certainly equal, if not better, than the other
candidates she had been considering. And though she
had only talked in depth with him for a couple of hours
today, an immediate bond had been created between
them.

As she watched Jim now, nervously fidgeting while
preparing to tape the appeal, she began thinking about
a proposal which, if it worked out, would be a large
step towards helping them both. She was developing
this idea as she went to the food table and poured
herself a coffee.

"Excuse me, Ms. Greenfield," interrupted Jim, "I
just want to thank you again for the food, the
phones...well, everything you've done. It's really
helped us get this whole procedure up and running
faster than we ever hoped for."

"It's your plan, Jim. Yours and Susan's. I'm just
along to be of whatever assistance I can," said Ms.
Greenfield.

"I don't know how I can ever return the kindness."

"Well, I do," she replied.

"Name it," said Jim. "I'd be willing to climb a
mountain for you."

"Oh, it's not that hard. When this situation is over and Travis is home safe and sound, I'd like to meet with you again, at my office. We're opening a new division, and I'm interested in discussing a management position with you. It will be hard work, but I've got a strong feeling that this challenge could be the right opportunity for you."

Jim was stunned. This was absolutely the last thing on his mind, and he was overwhelmed by the offer. "I'm flattered...I'm flabbergasted...and I most definitely would be interested in hearing about it."

"Good. Then not another word until we meet. The priority for now is finding Travis."

"Excuse me," interrupted one of the television crew. "We're about ready to start. Could you please join your wife and daughter."

"Sure, right away," replied Jim, nodding to Ms. Greenfield. He walked across the room with renewed vigour.

"Now, remember," said Jim to Susan and Natalie, as he sat beside them, "it's important that we don't look sad or angry. So let's have big smiles and lots of confidence when we read our statements."

"Okay, Daddy. Do you think Ogilthorpe has told Santa about Travis yet?" Natalie had been giving this lots of thought all day, and her enthusiasm continued to grow. "Maybe he's at the house right now looking for me, and I'm not there." This possibility caused her great concern, and she knotted her forehead with worry.

Susan recognized this inherited trait and gently squeezed her daughter's hand to reassure her. "Don't worry about that, honey. If Santa wants to know where you are, he'll find you."

"That's right, young lady, because...*He sees you when you're sleeping. He knows when you're awake...*" Jim sang and then tickled his daughter until her forehead relaxed and her laughter filled the room. Everyone looked over and smiled at this brief moment of normalcy.

"All right, people!" cued the cameraman. "We're ready to do a run-through as we discussed. Silence please...and rolling!"

Travis rolled over on the lumpy mattress and moaned as the muscles in his arms and shoulders pleaded for more rest. He had nearly collapsed from exhaustion the night before, immediately after downing another sandwich and soft drink.

His first day had been a long, difficult experience, and he remembered thinking that it couldn't get worse. Yet now, as he lay staring at the peeling paint on the ceiling in his room, he realized that today would be worse because he was so sore.

He had finished the third floor hallway and stairs and most of the second floor hall. Cuthbert MacIntyre had yelled at him a couple of times for no reason other than to remind him who was boss. Travis had tried his best not to get the old man angry and would continue those efforts today.

He wondered what Natalie was doing right now and if she was missing him. Probably not, since he was always teasing her, he reasoned. Then his stomach grumbled, and he could almost taste one of his dad's special omelettes. It made him think about both his parents and how angry they must be at him for running away. Before he could continue this thought, the familiar clicking of the key in the door lock began. He shuddered at the thought of his kidnapper. The door opened and there he was again with soda and sandwich in hand.

"Okay, kid. I let you sleep in today, but don't think I'll be so nice every day." The truth was that Cuthbert had forgotten all about Travis and had just rolled over and continued sleeping until he finally felt the urge to eat something. It was only as he stumbled into the kitchen that he saw the pail and brush and remembered his young victim.

"Here's something to eat. You got five minutes to use the bathroom and then be ready to finish the walls and floors. Move it!" He tossed the soda and sandwich at Travis and disappeared back into the kitchen.

Travis appeared in four minutes and immediately went to fill the bucket, saying not a word. He wanted to get into the hallway as fast as possible to get away from the old man's cigarette smoke, which irritated his eyes.

The rest of the day went as Travis expected. He worked, and Cuthbert supervised and napped. The task was made somewhat less dangerous when they started using the step ladder. Cuthbert had taken him to the basement storage area to retrieve it during the afternoon.

He seemed to be relaxing his guard, and Travis was constantly watching and studying, waiting for the right opportunity to make his escape. That time finally came late in the afternoon. The washing of the walls and floors in the hallways was finished. Travis had suggested he do maintenance on the overhead lights, dismantling them, washing the shades and replacing the worn-out bulbs where necessary. This enthusiasm had impressed Cuthbert, and he had readily agreed to it. He was now quite pleased with himself and the training of his young assistant. Resuming his familiar position at the base of the first staircase, he was planning the next day's chores as he nodded off.

Travis felt that this was the best chance he would get, and he readied himself for what was to follow. He had tested Cuthbert's sensitivity to sounds earlier by banging the brush in the pail and watching his reaction. Other than a snort and a slight shuffle, it did not affect him. So as soon as Travis heard the now familiar wheezing, he focussed on the front door locks. He planned to carefully ease down the stairs, stepping over the dozing man, and silently go to the front door. Starting at the top, he would unlatch the three locks and open the door, then head into the street, running like he'd never run before.

Everything was going perfectly as he approached Cuthbert, who cooperated by snoring quite loudly, giving Travis added confidence. But when he was right beside the man, it became obvious that it was impossible to just step over him, making it necessary to jump from the third step to the entrance hall floor and then run for the door.

Travis' heart was pounding as he took two deep breaths, then placed his left foot on the stair to launch his flight to freedom. He was in mid-air and his foot was just rising from the stair when he heard the loud creaking noise caused by the old hardwood flooring. Loosened by the passage of time, it sounded like an alarm.

This was all that was needed to rouse Cuthbert from his slumber. Startled by the sight of legs flying in front of his face, he raised his hands in an unconscious reflex and grabbed onto Travis' left ankle.

The force of the boy's momentum pulled Cuthbert

from the step, but he still managed to keep his grip. Travis tried to maintain his balance and, hopping on his other leg, he pulled and jerked his left foot, but to no avail. He finally fell over onto the floor in the front entrance.

Cuthbert was fully awake now and furious that his version of trust and kindness was being rejected so rudely. He pulled Travis towards him, and grabbing his shirt collar, yanked him up off the floor.

"So that's the thanks I get for saving your life, is it?" he yelled. "I can see now that I've been way too nice to ya'. But that's gonna change."

They went up the stairs to the apartment and back into Travis' room, where Cuthbert shoved the boy into the small closet. "That's the perfect place for you to stay and think about how bad you've been," said Cuthbert. "I'm going to the store for some smokes and food. You better think up a good apology while I'm gone."

He slammed the closet door shut, repeating the gesture with the bedroom door before locking it with the key from his shirt pocket. Grabbing his coat off the chair, he stormed out of the apartment, and Travis could hear him as he stomped down the stairs and out the front door.

The only sound now was the television. As his eyes adjusted to the darkness of the closet, Travis became aware of a small hole in the wall that let in a bit of light from the living room.

His foot touched something, and he squinted his eyes in the dim light until he realized it was his knapsack. He pulled it closer and opened it up, wanting to occupy his mind with something other than his failed escape attempt. Reaching in, he found the small flashlight, pulled it out, and turned it on to help identify the other contents. The clothes all smelled so nice and fresh, reminding him of home and his family.

He thought his mind was playing tricks on him when he began hearing his father's voice. He shook his head, as if trying to wake himself up and clear away the dream, but he still heard it. He finally figured out that it was coming from the television. Bending forward, he leaned against the wall and peered through the hole. He was just able to see the television screen, and his heart started pounding when he recognized his parents and sister.

"...I therefore would like to say once more that we love you very much, son, and want you to come back home. We need you to help finish putting up the Christmas decorations. We're sorry about the disagreement we had, and we'd like to put it behind us. So if you're able, please call us. And if anyone has Travis or knows where he is, please, please let him come home to his family. He is a very special boy, and we miss him dearly." The camera zoomed in on Jim's face and followed a tear as it ran down his cheek.

The picture widened to show all three Kirkland family members, then panned off to one side for the sign-off from the reporter.

"Anyone with any information can call the number shown on the bottom of the screen. Volunteers are here at the arena and also helping authorities conduct neighbourhood searches. This is Donald Mills, on location at the search party headquarters for missing 10-year-old Travis Kirkland. We now return to our regularly scheduled holiday program."

Travis sat back on the floor and waved the flashlight in jubilation. His biggest fears had been erased, and he was now even more intent on escaping his captivity.

"Yay-y!" he yelled. "They still love me and want me to come home." He tried to clap his hands but, still holding the flashlight, he instead stomped the floor with his feet and pounded the wall with his free hand. He leaned back to catch his breath and listened again to the television. The singer on the holiday musical special was performing "Silver Bells", and Travis loudly joined in for a chorus. He then remembered stuffing the small bell into the knapsack and rummaged through the clothes until he found it.

"Oh, little bell. We're going to get out of here and get home for a real Christmas with people I love and who love me. And I'll never run away again, because that doesn't solve anything. Gee, I wish I was home right now."

And then, in time to the music, he began to ring the bell. As before, he was enthralled by the purity of the sound. It encouraged him to ring it a second time, then a third time and then many more times, as he was filled with hope and determination. Best of all, he had a renewed faith in the spirit of Christmas.

Ogilthorpe dropped the jar of black polish onto the straw covering the stable floor and stood up straight. He was in the middle of demonstrating to the apprentices how to polish and shine the reindeer's hooves. It would be one of the last things done before the final harnessing for the big trip. As usual, Dasher was his volunteer model.

"Did anyone perchance hear that?" he asked.

The other elves looked at each other and shrugged their little shoulders. "Hear what?" replied Mortimer, acting as spokes-elf.

But Ogilthorpe had already heard the bell ringing the second and third times. As he dashed from the stall and out of the stable, he managed to call out to the others, "Class dismissed!"

He ran across the courtyard, clicking the heels on his elf boots and loudly proclaiming for all to hear,

"It's the missing sleigh bell! It's been rung again!" He dashed up the steps to the workshop and burst in, pausing momentarily to take a deep breath.

His dramatic entrance caught everyone's attention, and the normal hustle and bustle of the place stopped. Santa was in his leather chair by the fireplace, warming his toes and finalizing his list. He began to smile in anticipation of Ogilthorpe's news.

"Well, my friend, to what do we owe the pleasure of your company?" he teased.

"I heard it, Santa. The missing bell was rung three times. In fact, it was rung many wonderful, beautiful, enchanting times!" Ogilthorpe tended to get carried away when he got excited.

"Well then," said Santa, getting out of his chair and stepping into his slippers, "let's take a look to see what's going on."

He walked over to the window and opened it. This time he picked up some loose snow and made a new snowball. Ogilthorpe was so excited that the tips of his ears were already vibrating to the frequency of the bell. Santa needed only to watch the snowball begin to glow and then crystallize. He was very pleased as the image began to form and he was able to recognize that it was indeed Travis Kirkland.

"Great boughs of holly, it looks like Travis has not only found the Christmas spirit but feels it even stronger than before. Quite remarkable! Hm-m-m. Now, to figure out where he is."

Santa had developed this ability to locate people as they started travelling more to spend Christmas with family or friends. It was nice when children mentioned in their letters that they'd be away, but sometimes they were so excited that they forgot or their parents surprised them with last-minute trips.

He concentrated hard and stared intently at Travis' image.

"Oh my, my, my...it couldn't be...but, yes, I believe it is. It's Cuthbert MacIntyre! Now, that is someone we haven't heard from in a long, long time. Wouldn't you know it! Somebody who stopped believing in Christmas before he even reached nursery school ends up being the cause of all this unhappiness. Well, there's no time to waste. Ogilthorpe, please get the sleigh ready...team of eight, in harness, for an emergency trip."

"Right away, Santa!" Ogilthorpe immediately headed for the door, grabbing a handful of candy canes out of habit.

As he left the workshop, he noticed the courtyard beginning to fill with elves. Word of the ringing bell had spread quickly, and everyone was anxious to know what was happening.

"Ogilthorpe!" called out Dudley. "Was it the missing bell? Does Travis still have it?"

"Yes, and yes," replied a running Ogilthorpe. "Santa is going on a special flight. I must get the reindeer and sleigh ready!"

The stable apprentices and other elves who had done service in the stable all worked together. In no time at all, the sleigh was out and ready with the eight reindeer harnessed and set to take off. The elves had never been so rushed, but their training and skills really shone through.

Santa was most impressed as he walked across the yard and saw they were waiting for him. He was pulling on his mittens as he approached the sleigh.

"Ho-ho-ho...wonderful...wonderful!" he exclaimed. All the elves gathered around and cheered. "All right, everybody, everything else is still on schedule. This trip shouldn't take too long. In the meantime, let's make sure that all the usual details are attended to, so that we'll be ready for another grand Christmas. The children are counting on us!" He knew the elves wouldn't let him or the children down. "It's time to go. Come on, Ogilthorpe. I may need your help. I promise not to fly too high and no loop-de-loops. Ho-ho-ho!"

Santa laughed, and all the elves giggled and applauded as Ogilthorpe bravely stepped into the sleigh and crawled under the polar bear skin rug that Santa used to keep warm. One quick whistle from Santa and the reindeer pulled the sleigh effortlessly along the snow. When they had gathered enough speed he whistled again, and Dasher led the reindeer into the evening sky.

Ogilthorpe's eyes were closed, and he decided they should stay that way. Maybe he would even have a little snooze during the trip.

The moon was almost full and glowed brightly as they sped past it. The harnesses on the reindeer glistened in response.

"You've done an excellent job with the team, Ogilthorpe," complimented Santa. "That was one of the smoothest takeoffs I can remember."

"Thank you, Santa. We've been doing a lot of practising during the last few weeks. I'm glad you noticed." Then peeking over the edge, he saw the lights of a city far below. "This is still pretty far north for a city that size, isn't it, Santa?"

"We're not that far north anymore. That's our destination."

"Our destination...but, but, we only left a little while ago!"

"Don't forget...eight reindeer are better than one. And besides, I know a little shortcut around the moon." Santa winked and chuckled while Ogilthorpe stared, astonished as the city below drew closer.

The swirling snowfall that surrounded the sleigh intensified as they descended onto the roof of Cuthbert MacIntyre's building. The early evening darkness provided additional coverage as they came to a stop in the moon shadow of the chimney.

Santa had developed a basic plan on the trip down, and he surveyed the street below to confirm his recollections.

"Ah, yes. There still is a fire hydrant across the street. That should provide the necessary means to attract a little attention," he said.

Ogilthorpe stood beside Santa, not knowing or understanding what he was doing, but believing totally that it would do the trick. Santa picked up some snow and made a loose snowball. Then aiming carefully, he threw it down at the hydrant.

The snowball hit the top of the hydrant and burst into a million snowflakes. They began to swirl around the hydrant, completely covering it with a sparkling, icy layer, which ran all the way to the bottom. It continued down the pipe, into the ground and right to the main water line, which flowed below.

The chilling effect of this quick freezing resulted in a solid block of ice, strangling the rushing water and causing it to be diverted up the smaller pipe to the hydrant. This caused tremendous pressure and made the cap break apart, releasing a fountain of water that surged high into the air.

A snowplow was coming up the street, and it radioed in a burst water main signal to the emergency road crews.

"That was a very good throw, Santa. Have you been practising?" kidded Ogilthorpe.

"Ho-ho-ho! It helps to stay in shape," he replied. "Now, that is taken care of. Let's go and see what else we can do."

Holding the end of Ogilthorpe's cap, Santa concentrated as a swirl of snow surrounded them. Then touching the side of his nose with his finger and nodding his head, they began to rise from the roof. They floated over the edge and then descended the outside of the building. Suspended in midair, they peered into the apartment's living room through the window.

Cuthbert MacIntyre had returned earlier with his purchases and had not spoken with Travis yet. He went to unlock the bedroom door, not realizing he was now being watched.

"I'm back, kid. Here's your dinner." He tossed in a couple of stale buns he'd bought at the convenience store. "I don't know why I'm being so nice to you," he growled.

"You must be getting the Christmas spirit, just like me!" exclaimed Travis, as he caught the buns.

"Hah, not likely. Christmas is just for kids. And you're too old to believe in that stuff."

"You're wrong. Christmas is for everyone. It's the best time of the year, and even my mom and dad believe in Christmas. They're going to find me, and you are going to be in big trouble!"

"...and you are going to be in big trouble," mimicked Cuthbert. "I don't have to listen to this garbage. So clam up and get some rest. Tomorrow you start working really hard!" He slammed the door and locked it, placing the key back into his shirt pocket. He returned to the kitchen and sat at the table with his back facing Travis' room. He began to eat a bowl of soup.

Ogilthorpe was watching carefully when he noticed Travis' eye appear at the hole in the wall.

"Look, Santa. Travis is watching Cuthbert too. From the small hole in the wall, beside the door."

"That gives me an idea," said Santa. "If he's as smart as I believe him to be, then we might just be able to help him escape on his own."

Santa looked back at Cuthbert, slowly stirring the soup with his spoon. Carefully pointing his finger, Santa concentrated hard and, in an instant, the liquid in Cuthbert's bowl was frozen solid with the spoon still in it.

Cuthbert squinted his eyes, then leaned forward. The bowl was frozen to the table, and he could not move it.

"Hey, what's going on?" he exclaimed, grabbing the bowl. With both hands around it and his feet planted firmly on the floor, he yanked at the frozen mass until it finally broke free. But the force of his movement pushed him back in his chair, and he toppled backwards onto the floor, hitting his head.

The key to Travis' room was flung from his shirt

pocket and slid across the floor. It was beginning to slow down when Santa waved his hand, and a thin layer of ice formed a pathway which led right under the door and into Travis' room.

Travis had seen the key sliding towards him, and he wasted no time in grabbing his knapsack, getting out of the closet and picking up the key. He didn't know if Cuthbert was still on the floor, but this didn't stop him from unlocking the bedroom door and running for the apartment doorway.

Stunned by the blow to his head and the fall to the floor, Cuthbert was slowly coming to his senses when he heard Travis open the apartment door to the hallway. He stood up in time to see the young boy dash out, slamming the door behind him. Cuthbert stumbled after him, but to his surprise, the doorknob was covered with ice, thanks to Santa. So, grabbing an old walking cane from the hall stand, he smacked it against the knob, breaking the ice and allowing him to open the door. He ran into the hallway, intent on recapturing his victim.

Santa and Ogilthorpe had magically entered the building and were positioned at the top of the third floor staircase. They were able to see right down into the front hall where Travis was frantically undoing the three locks on the front door.

Cuthbert paused at the top of the staircase and yelled down, "You won't get very far, kid. I think it's time to teach you a good lesson!" He shook the cane in the air and took one step forward. Before he could react, his foot was sliding off the layer of ice with which Santa had covered the whole staircase. He fell onto his backside and began a bumpy, swift descent on the stairs.

Travis was releasing the third and final lock as Cuthbert neared the bottom. The youngster wasted no time in swinging open the door and running across the front porch. Cuthbert was still in pursuit, but not in control, as he continued sliding across the floor and right through the open doorway.

"Yie-e-e-e!" he screamed when he realized he was headed straight for the metal handrail. He came to a very uncomfortable stop with his legs straddling it and his extended tongue firmly stuck to the ice-cold metal.

Travis was only halfway down the front stairs when he started calling out. "Help! Help me! I've been kidnapped!" he screamed. He stopped after looking around, realizing he was now quite safe.

Standing right across the street was Officer Lynn Douglas and four members of the road and water departments. They had responded to the frozen water main alarm and had just arrived with their equipment.

"Say, isn't that the lost boy we saw on T.V.?" asked one of the workers.

"Looks like him to me," said another.

They rushed over to his side, as Officer Douglas

radioed for additional police to come. She had no doubt in her mind that it was Travis, having memorized his photo. She was greatly relieved to see him in person.

"Well, Travis, you've certainly had a lot of people concerned about where you've been," she said.

"It was him," replied Travis, pointing to the pathetic figure frozen to the railing at the top of the stairs. "He kidnapped me and tried to make me his slave!"

"Well, now," said Officer Douglas, climbing the steps towards Cuthbert. "Didn't your parents ever tell you not to put your tongue onto frozen metal?"

"Ah-h-h-h, ya-a-a-a!" he mumbled, unable to form words in his current predicament.

"Save it for the judge, sir!" she instructed as she immediately handcuffed his wrists behind his back.

Another police car arrived, and the policemen had a good laugh at the sight of Cuthbert still stuck to the railing. Officer Douglas instructed them to take over.

"Can you please process this guy? I've got an important delivery to make." She gently put her arm around Travis' shoulders and guided him over to her patrol car and out of the cold night air.

Santa and Ogilthorpe had watched the whole thing from the shadows of the front hallway and were pleased to see it turn out so well. Ogilthorpe was anxious to retrieve the bell, and he started vibrating his ear tips to get a response from it.

"I believe our young friend took the bell with him." said Santa.

"Oh, my goodness! What will we do now?" said Ogilthorpe.

"Why don't we let him keep the bell," replied Santa. "The most important thing was to help rescue Travis, and we've managed to do that. So let's get back to the sleigh..."

And in the blink of an eye, they were standing on the roof beside the reindeer.

"All in all, it was a job well done, Ogilthorpe," said Santa, climbing into the sleigh. "Now it's time to get back home and help with the final preparations for this year's big trip."

"I guess you're right, Santa." He paused, thinking about Natalie's special belief and Travis' renewed faith in the magic of Christmas. "No, I'm sure you are right. Travis and Natalie will be wonderful guardians of the sleigh bell," declared Ogilthorpe as he crawled under the warm fur blanket. "But do you think we could make one more stop before heading back, please?"

The reindeer responded to Santa's silent command with the reins, and they quickly moved forward and up into the sky as Ogilthorpe explained what he wished to do.

Jim and Susan had reluctantly agreed to leave the rescue headquarters. They had been there for most of the day and, at the insistence of all the volunteers, they left to take Natalie home to bed. She was still brimming with confidence that her friend from the North Pole was going to help find Travis. Anxiously, she ran ahead of her parents and opened the door to the house. She quickly removed her boots, then ran up to her room with her coat still on.

Jim and Susan paused on the porch and looked back across the front yard. The snow from the storm was still fluffy and white, and their neighbours' yards were glowing with Christmas decorations. Any other time they would have marvelled at the sight, but now they hardly even noticed.

"I hope he's all right," said Susan.

"I'm sure he is," replied Jim. "It's a feeling I've got that I can't explain...but I know he is okay."

He had no sooner said this when they noticed the flashing lights. It looked as if someone's Christmas display had gone haywire, and they realized it was a police car only when it reached the house. As soon as the car came to a stop, the passenger door flew open, and Travis jumped out.

"Mom! Dad!" he called, running up the walk to the porch.

"Travis!" yelled Jim, his face breaking into the biggest smile he had ever had.

"Oh, honey, you're okay," said Susan. She bent down and opened her arms wide as her son ran directly into her embrace. He dropped his knapsack, and the contents partly spilled onto the porch, but no one even noticed. "You are okay, aren't you?"

"I'm okay now, Mom. Some creepy guy took me to his apartment and tried to make me do all sorts of dumb chores around his building. But the whole time I was there, I was trying to get away. And when I saw you guys on T.V., and you weren't angry with me...well, I just kept trying, until I escaped."

"Pardon me, folks." It was Officer Douglas. She had followed Travis up the path. "We've taken the man into custody, and we'll need a full statement from Travis. But it can wait until tomorrow morning. I'm sure you've got some catching up to do."

"Thank you, Officer, you did a great job," said Jim.

"To be honest with you, sir, it was just luck. I was checking a broken water main, and it was like...like magic, the way Travis came running out of a building just as I was standing there."

"It was magic!" exclaimed Natalie, who had come back out onto the porch. "Santa magic!"

The adults chuckled, and the officer smiled as she said goodnight and went back to her car. The family was standing on the porch hugging each other and waving to the officer as the vehicle pulled away.

Travis started thinking. "You know, it was kind of like magic the way the key to the room I was in just slid under the door to me."

"And the candy canes!" said Natalie.

"Candy canes. What candy canes?" asked her father.

"These ones!" she exclaimed proudly, handing out one to each of them. She had found them on her pillow in her room.

That was the quick stop Ogilthorpe had asked Santa to make before returning to the North Pole.

"I'll bet Santa was here and left them just for us."

Jim looked at Susan and silently motioned to the candy canes they now held. She shook her head slowly, then motioned back to him and received the same bewildered denial.

"Well, anyway, I'm glad it's all over. And to celebrate, we're going to buy whatever toys you wished for for Christmas," proclaimed Jim.

Travis didn't hesitate for a second and replied, "I've already got what I wished for, and that was to be back home with all of you, celebrating Christmas like always."

Natalie saw the sleigh bell laying on top of Travis' sweater on the porch. She quickly picked it up and showed it to everyone. "Travis, did you have this when you made a wish to be back home?"

"Uh-h, yeah. I was holding it and even ringing it a little."

"Then you really do believe in the magic of Christmas, and Santa was able to come and help you. You see, you've got to believe for the magic to work."

"I've never believed in it more than I do right now," declared Travis.

"You too, Mommy, Daddy. Do you believe?" questioned Natalie.

"Yes, honey. I've always believed," replied Susan.

"I may have forgotten how to believe for a little while, but I'm the most believing dad in the whole city," proclaimed Jim.

With that, Natalie rang the bell, and for the first time her parents heard the special sound it made. They stood in silence appreciating the beauty of its song.

Suddenly, in the distance, they heard a similar sound...not from just one sleigh bell, but from many. Everyone turned and looked up to the sky. Nothing seemed out of the ordinary. Aside from the moon and the stars, a few clouds dotted the heavens.

Then they noticed a swirling mass of snow crossing in front of the moon. The wonderful sound seemed to be coming from that direction.

"An airplane?" asked Susan.

"I don't think so," said Travis.

"Maybe an echo," suggested Jim.

"Maybe a special friend," heralded Natalie, as she

continued ringing the bell. "Merry Christmas, Santa!" she called out, waving and shouting. "Thank you, Ogilthorpe! Merry, Merry Christmas!"

Enriched by the magic of that moment, they all lingered on the porch listening to the sound of bells fading into the distance.

The magic sleigh bell was put in a place of honour on the fireplace mantel that night. Inspired by the bell, the whole family together completed the decorating and began their celebration.

This was going to be the best Christmas they had ever had.

The End

Merry Christmas